THE
APACHE
FIGHTER

THE
APACHE
FIGHTER

WILL
COOK

THORNDIKE
CHIVERS

This Large Print edition is published by Thorndike Press®, Waterville, Maine USA and by BBC Audiobooks Ltd, Bath, England.

Published in 2006 in the U.S. by arrangement with Golden West Literary Agency.

Published in 2006 in the U.K. by arrangement with Golden West Literary Agency.

U.S. Hardcover ISBN   0-7862-8797-7   (Western)
U.K. Hardcover ISBN 10 1 4056 3866 4   (Chivers Large Print)
U.K. Hardcover ISBN 13 978 1 405 63866 1
U.K. Softcover ISBN 10 1 4056 3867 2   (Camden Large Print)
U.K. Softcover ISBN 13 978 1 405 63867 8

The text of this Large Print edition is unabridged.
Other aspects of the book may vary from the original edition.

Set in 16 pt. Plantin.

Printed in the United States on permanent paper.

British Library Cataloguing-in-Publication Data available

Library of Congress Cataloging-in-Publication Data

Cook, Will.
    The Apache fighter / by Will Cook.
        p. cm. — (Thorndike Press large print Westerns)
    ISBN 0-7862-8797-7 (lg. print : hc : alk. paper)
    1. Apache Indians — Fiction.   2. Large type books.
  I. Title.   II. Series: Thorndike Press large print Western
series.
PS3553.O5547A87 2006
  813′.54—dc22   2006010062

THE
APACHE
FIGHTER

In Tucson, in 1872, the one-story adobe Buckalew Block was considered the cultural center of town, the rest being mostly Mexican, Papago Indians, no-account whites and army people, which more or less indicates how the social scale ran.

People talked about the heat and the dust and whether or not the military would ever get that telegraph line strung between San Diego and Sante Fe, and if they did, how long the Apaches would leave it up.

The Southern Overland Stage Company hadn't run regularly since 1861, and although the line offered triple pay to drivers for that stretch from Lordsburg — through Apache Pass, Camp Bowie and Benson to Tucson — there were few takers. Occasionally the army would take a troop through as a coach escort for an arriving officer or visitor of importance, but travel on an organized scale did not exist.

Except for Sergeant Joe Moses, who made the run from Tucson to Lordsburg every six days. He carried mail and the dispatches brought down to Tucson from Camp Lowell, delivered packages to the stage relay stations and the few ranches along the way, and now and then he took a passenger with him in his buggy, making the trip with the regularity of a good watch. For this duty he drew thirty-six dollars and twenty-five cents a month.

Although Sergeant Moses was a young man, barely twenty-eight, he was halfway through his third hitch with ten years of service, commencing as a drummer boy in an Ohio regiment and later transferring to the cavalry, a branch of service more suited to his temperament.

He was the size and weight the cavalry liked, about five-ten and weighing a hundred and sixty pounds which beef and beans and hard-bread and countless patrols had pared to *caliche* hardness. Moses' skin was the color of copper, yet his hair was fair and his eyes were blue. He always wore his hat tipped forward on his head, the band resting just above his eyebrows.

He wore two heavy .44 Smith & Wesson pistols and a knife big enough to serve as a hatchet; in his buggy, mounted to the dashboard, were two eight-gauge sawed-off shotguns, butts within easy grabbing distance. His duty gave him a freedom of

8

dress not usually granted to military men. Moses often wore no uniform shirt; to him merely hoisting his suspenders over his red underwear, tying his neckerchief and tugging his hat in place was the uniform of the day.

Officers newly arrived from the east, where regulations are regulations, frowned at this display of originality and whimsy, but no one had ever been able to do anything about it. One rash lieutenant confined Moses to the post for three days and when Colonel Spencer, who commanded Camp Bowie, failed to get his cigars on time, a company was dispatched to trace down the source of this delay.

The lieutenant was transferred to Fort Yuma, and Sergeant Joe Moses departed in his buggy for his regularly appointed rounds, hat cast low over his eyes and the sleeves of his red underwear rolled halfway up his forearms.

On the eastbound run, the stage relay station twenty miles from Lordsburg was a particular favorite of Joe Moses. He arrived at noon, during the worst heat of the day, and while his horses were being changed, he took off his heavy cartridge belt, laid his revolvers on the stone trough curbing, climbed in and sat in the water, cooling himself and killing the self-generated aroma of five and a half unwashed days.

Through with his bath, he poured the water from his boots, rebuckled his belt and walked over to his buggy where Abe Wichles was waiting. He was an elderly man, round in the stomach and nearly toothless, and ran the station with three helpers and four Mexican hostlers.

"See any Injuns?" Wichles asked.

Joe Moses shook his head.

"I ain't seen none either," Wichles said. "Watch for 'em though. Ain't nothin' else to do around here." He looked at the mountains and the desert. "You hear when another coach is comin' through? Been a month now."

Moses said, "The old man at Bowie said he had to go to Lordsburg in a couple weeks. He may take a company. You can bring a stage through then." He got in his buggy and lifted the reins. "You want anything on the way back?"

"Somethin' to read," Wichles said. Then he thought of something and put his hand up to Moses' arm. "Say, there was a fella through here two days ago, westbound. You run into him?"

Moses shook his head. "He never showed at Camp Bowie."

Wichles pressed his lips into a rubbery mass. "Damn! Told him to wait. Some fellas know it all. Well, you never *see* 'Paches, but they see you." He stepped back and slapped the near horse on the rump with his hat, and Sergeant Moses stormed out of the yard.

He gave the horses a quarter of a mile to kick out the ginger, then pulled them to a walk. He wrapped the reins loosely around the whip socket, propped a boot against the dashboard and studied the vast shimmering sweep of desert. Distant mountains piled high against the sky and the desert dropped away in a steady down slope as he rode along in the bake-oven heat, the buggy top affording him only a poor shade at best.

Moses gave a detailed study to each clump of mesquite, each greasewood bush, and then took one of the shotguns and held it across his lap. He rode on in this posture of relaxed vigilance.

Although Sergeant Joe Moses made this run every six days, he had seen only four Apaches, and that had been four years ago. It had been his first trip and he had been feeling jumpy anyway. He didn't like the

11

canyons with their sheer walls and echoes and he'd just been approaching the end of one when they popped up at him.

One had fired too quickly and that gave Moses his chance; he cut the Apache down with his shotgun, jumped out of the buggy and fired at another who was charging him with a knife raised.

Two got away. Two lay dead. He had looked at them and had seen that they had been very young and very brave and certainly foolish, but then the young and the brave were that way.

After that he never saw another Apache, but they saw him and he knew it. They watched him each time he came through and waited for him to forget, to relax, to make a mistake. It was a deadly game he played with Chief Cochise and his Apaches, with rules that each side followed carefully.

Joe Moses didn't enjoy the game, but he played it because it was his job.

Now he could see Lordsburg in the distance. He reached the outskirts just before sunset when the last light of day played against the bare face of the town. It was laid out in a line, along one street that opened up to the vast reach of the desert. The dying sun made blood squares of the

12

windows and painted the wood and adobe buildings a dark wine color.

Moses put up at the livery stable, parked the buggy around in back in a lean-to and turned the horses into a corral made of slender gnarled poles hammered into the stubborn ground. He took his shotguns and locked them, along with his pistols and knife, in the metal express box the farrier sergeant at Camp Lowell had built under the seat.

The leather dispatch case and mail sack tucked under his arm, Joe Moses walked toward the center of town and the stage office. Harry Spears was behind the counter; he smiled and said, "How's everything down the line?"

"Quiet." Moses put the sack and dispatch case on the counter. "The mail you can sort. Dispatches go to Sante Fe." He turned his neckerchief around and wiped sweat off his face. Dirt lay as mud in the creases of his skin and his beard stubble itched. "I'll pick up the sacks in the morning."

"All right," Spears said. "Joe, is the army doin' anything about Cochise?"

"What do you think they ought to do?" Moses asked.

Spears raised his shoulders and let them

drop. He was a bland man, thirty some, with a celluloid collar and a pink-and-white-striped shirt.

"Everything's come to a standstill," Spears said. "The hotel's crowded with folks wanting to get through to points west. There ain't been a stage through now in —"

"I know when the last one went through," Moses said dryly. "Colonel Spencer may come through in a couple of weeks with a company."

"Well, that's something anyway," Spears said.

Moses went out and looked up and down the street. Riders moved up and down and the boardwalk fronting the stores carried a thick traffic. He turned and walked toward the hotel. Many spoke to him and he nodded or waved but did not stop, not even at the saloon which was a part of the hotel.

A short alley, a wagon-wide gap, separated the saloon from the rest of the row of buildings and Joe Moses stepped across it to the barbershop. There was a customer in the chair, but he was almost done, so Moses sat down to wait.

"Who's in the bath?" Moses asked, nodding toward the rear of the building.

"George Howard," the barber said.

"He'll be out in a few minutes. I've got the boy drawing clean water."

"There'll be mud in the bottom of the tub when I get through," Moses said.

One of the other customers said, "Sergeant, you just about own that road now, don't you?"

"Cochise owns it," Joe Moses admitted. "He just lets me use it." George Howard came out, radiating the aroma of toilet water. He patted the ruffles on the front of his shirt and carefully put on his derby, studying the precise angle in the barber's mirror. Moses said, "George, why don't you use the tub at your hotel?"

"It costs a dollar and a half," Howard said, smiling. "With two tubs in town, there's a price war going on."

There was a commotion outside and they all stepped to the window to look out. Two riders came storming down the street, their ropes tied to a wagon tongue. The wagon careened wildly from side to side and the men yelled and kicked their horses until finally the wagon veered onto the walk and smashed halfway through a store front.

George Howard paid the barber and said, "We're going to have a night of it. Jim and Pete Ketchel have come to town."

15

A crowd was converging on the wrecked store and the two men cast their ropes off the saddles and swung into the nearest hitch rack.

"Come over later," Howard said. "I'll buy you a drink, Joe."

"All right," Moses said and went into the back room for his bath. The Mexican boy was filling the tub and he had a clean uniform laid out for Moses, who kept clothes at both ends of the line.

"I clean your boots, Señor Joe," the boy said and took them away.

Moses lingered in the bath. It was a luxury he didn't want to waste; he had very few and enjoyed them all. He lathered and rinsed and dried himself and now and then he heard the Ketchel boys whooping it up; there was some shooting and a lot of yelling but no one paid any attention to it.

He dressed and went out into the shop in his stocking feet; the boy hadn't brought his boots back. The barber was holding the chair open and Moses sagged into it; the barber dropped him flat and lathered his face.

"How was the bath, Joe?"

"Gets better all the time," Moses admitted.

One of the customers said dryly, "Charlie, how come he gets a free bath and a shave?"

"You make the ride and I'll give you a free bath and a shave," the barber said.

"Thanks, I'd rather pay for mine."

Boots thumped along the walk and the door banged open and Pete Ketchel jerked the apron off Joe Moses and said, "Come on, you're sittin' where I want to sit."

Moses unwound the hot towel from his face and sat up; he looked at Pete Ketchel and at his brother, Jim, who stood just inside the door. "Is that a fact?"

Pete Ketchel had started something that pride told him to finish and good sense told him to leave alone. He wiped a hand across his mouth and said, "I didn't recognize you without your boots, Joe. No harm done."

He was the older, thirty, dressed in a torn shirt and worn leather breeches; he wore a pistol on each hip and had been known to shoot both at the same time, with considerable accuracy.

Jim Ketchel said, "We can come back, Pete. I'm thirsty."

"I guess that's best," Pete admitted and backed out the door. They stood on the walk a moment, then both walked over to George Howard's saloon.

Joe Moses lay back and let the barber put another hot towel on his face. From the muffled folds, Moses said, "With two fellas hunting trouble like they do, it's a shame they don't find it."

"They're just high-spirited," the barber said.

"Yeah, and I've had horses that way," Moses said, "but I'll be damned if I'd let 'em kick the slats out of my buckboard."

The barber shaved him close, put on some toilet water, and the Mexican boy brought Moses his boots. He gave the boy a quarter and a pat on the head, then put on his hat and went out across the alleyway.

Howard's place was crowded when Moses tried to find a place at the bar; so when Howard called to him, he went over to his table and sat down. The Ketchel brothers were at the bar, laughing and drinking, and they watched them for a moment.

Then Howard said, "If we had a city marshal we might calm those two down."

"Is that what it would take?" Moses asked. He helped himself to Howard's bottle, downed his drink, and then sat there with the warm fire spreading in his stomach.

"You know," Howard said, "if I could get through like you do I'd be a rich man. Five hundred dollars a head, that's what I'd charge and there'd be a lot of people who'd pay it." He reached out and touched Joe Moses on the arm. "How do you do it, Joe?"

"I'm careful," Moses admitted.

Howard laughed and brushed his finger against his mustache. "Secret, huh? Well, keep it that way if you want. I don't blame you."

"No secret," Moses said. "Other men have made it."

"That's right. One out of eight or ten maybe. But you just go back and forth, back and forth. I'd like to know how you do that, Joe."

"Come along and find out."

Howard laughed and shook his head. "I'd rather you just told me."

"If you knew," Moses pointed out, "you'd still have to make the trip to find out if I'd told you the truth."

"It seems that a man just can't win," Howard said. "Well, I'll stay here and make money. As long as the stages don't run, passengers jam up here. Some stay a week, hoping the situation will change. Some stay longer. But most go back to Sante Fe or El Paso. Either way, they use my hotel and drink in my saloon and eat in my dining room." He took two cigars from his pocket and offered one to Moses, then a match. "When you go back in the morning, you may have a passenger."

"Who?"

Howard shrugged. "Take your choice. There's four I know of who've been waiting for you." He let a smile grow. "Two are pretty — and pretty careful with their money."

"The other two?"

"They're my kind," Howard admitted. "Men *with* money."

Moses got up. "Thanks for the drink. What's your cook servin' tonight?"

Howard thought a minute. "Stew, potatoes, canned tomatoes, and peach pie."

"That sounds good to me," Joe Moses said and went outside.

Darkness was deep now and lamps came on along the street; riders stirred up the dust and there was an air of frustrated impatience to the town.

The hotel dining room was next door and Moses went on in, took a table and sat down. There was no ordering; you took what was served, all you could eat for a dollar. He waited, listening to the babble of talk and the constant buzz of the flies. In an hour it would be cooler and the flies would be gone, but they'd be back at sunup.

The waiter brought his meal and he tasted the stew, finding it good; he wondered whether it really *was* good, or did it just taste that way after his palate had been numbed by dried meat and bread.

The dining room was crowded with people he didn't know, people stranded here, waiting for a stage to go through to Tucson, or waiting while they made up their mind about turning back. Miners in from their trackless wanderings a hundred miles south in Mexico ate alone, content to go it alone even in town. There were a few women, one to every fifteen men, matrons with their husbands and some with children.

Next door, a shot rang out, followed by breaking glass. Joe Moses supposed it was the Ketchel boys exercising their high spirits.

A woman came into the dining room; he appraised her, made his guess: tall, thirty some. She stopped, looked around, saw him and came on to his table.

"Sergeant Moses?"

He scraped back his chair and stood up. "Yes'm." She had a thin, narrow face, a straight nose and warm brown eyes; her hair was dark without a trace of gray.

"May I sit down, Sergeant? I'd like to talk to you."

He quickly came around the table and pulled a chair back for her and she smiled at him. When he sat down, she said, "My name is Mrs. Curry. I'm the schoolteacher for the new school in Tucson. Or I will be if I ever get there."

"And you want to ride with me in the morning," Moses said.

"Yes. Sergeant, this is August. School is supposed to start in September. A year and a half has been lost already."

"This is your first trip west?" he asked.

"Yes. I'm from Pennsylvania."

"It's different out here."

"Very different, Sergeant, will you take me with you to Tucson?"

"It's a six-day ride and I've never taken a woman," Moses said. "Mrs. Curry, I don't think you've got any idea how rough those six days can be." He looked at her a moment. "Where's your husband?"

"Dead. Three years ago." She leaned forward and folded her hands. "Sergeant, I've been informed that there are over thirty children in Tucson who have reached ten years old without one year of formal schooling. I think that's a shame, a real shame."

"Well, it's nothing to brag about," Moses admitted. He leaned back in his chair.

"Mrs. Curry, before I pull out in the morning, a half dozen people will come to me and give me good reasons why I should take them along. Some offer me money. Once a man offered me three hundred dollars, and I don't make much more than that in a year." He smiled. "Did the clerk tell you you could find me at this table?"

"Yes."

"That's because I sit here every time I come to Lordsburg. You could say that I hold a sort of court because people come to this table and tell me why they have to get to Tucson, or Yuma, or San Diego, and I listen and decide who'll go with me. It's not the kind of decision a man likes to make, but who else is goin' to make it?"

Mrs. Curry listened carefully, then said, "Sergeant, that man who offered you money — what did he do when you turned him down?"

"He pulled a pistol from under his coat," Moses said. "But the man behind him knocked it out of his hand, then tried to use that as a lever to get himself a ride. I turned him down too because any man who can think that fast will figure out some way to get along."

"You have quite a responsibility, Sergeant. Has anyone ever questioned it?"

He nodded and laughed. "Quite a few. Especially army wives who feel that their husband's rank entitles them to some privileges." He looked past her as a slender, well-dressed man approached. He wore a derby and he carried a cane and his watch chain would have been a bargain at a hundred dollars.

"Pull up a chair," Moses said pleasantly. The man smiled, and sat down, carefully removing his hat so as not to spoil the part in his hair.

"My name is Bill Kelly, Sergeant." He glanced at Mrs. Curry and nodded and smiled pleasantly. "I'll come right to the point. I have important business in Tucson."

Moses nodded and squinted his eyes, continuing his study of Bill Kelly. "It wouldn't have anything to do with that pair of pistols you're carrying under your coat, would it?"

Kelly laughed suddenly and said, "You're very observant, Sergeant. The fact that my business is important should be sufficient."

"I'd take that into consideration," Moses said. He quickly switched his glance to Mrs. Curry. "Who was the sixth president of the United States?"

"Why — I —" Color came to her face. "Is this an examination, Sergeant?"

"Yes, and I'm afraid you failed it," Moses said. "You're well tanned, Mrs. Curry, and there's a pale mark on your third finger, left hand. To me that sort of says you've taken a ring off recently. Yet you told me your husband's been dead three years." He smiled and scratched his cheek. "Now eastern ladies like their fine complexion and wear bonnets to protect it. An army wife —"

She sighed and nodded. "My husband is Captain Dane, Third Cavalry."

"I know him," Moses said. "Curry a maiden name?"

She nodded again. "I'm sorry, Sergeant. I thought I was being clever."

"You were. But where did you find out about the school teacher?"

"I read it in the Sante Fe paper last month," she said. "Well, I took my chances, didn't I?"

"Yes," Moses said. "I leave at six in the morning, Mrs. Dane. And I'll have to limit your baggage to a portmanteau."

She opened her mouth in surprise, then a smile made a bloom of her face and she took his hand and held it. "Sergeant, thank you. But would you tell me why? I did try to deceive you."

"You didn't have a chance," Moses said frankly. "I took the schoolteacher through on the last trip. It was a *he*."

She got up, hesitated, then hurried out.

Bill Kelly said, "What about me, friend?"

"What about you?" Moses asked. "What's your line? Cards or pistols? It sure as hell ain't work, not with those hands."

Kelly smiled without humor. "The army sticks together, doesn't it?"

"That wasn't my reason."

"It was to me."

"Think what you damned please," Moses said.

The stain of anger came into Bill Kelly's eyes and his expression grew hard. "You sit there like some damned god, telling a man what he can do and can't do. I don't have to like it and I sure don't."

"Suit yourself. You want to go to Tucson so bad, then get on a horse and go," Moses advised. "You wouldn't get through Apache Pass, friend. I'd make a bet on it." Kelly started to get up and Joe Moses put his hands solidly against the edge of the table. "You're thinking of something and I'll tell you now it won't work. You want to try it anyway?"

For a moment Kelly teetered, then he

made a disgusted cut with his hand, wheeled and walked out. As he got to the door and rudely bumped into a young woman who was entering, he changed his mind and came back to Moses' table.

"Suppose I just trail you through," Kelly said. "What's to stop me from doin' that?"

"Cochise," Moses said. "But you're welcome to try."

"I'll see you in the morning," Kelly said and wheeled, bumping into the woman again. "Can't you watch where you're going?" he asked and stalked out.

"The poor man's probably troubled by indigestion," the woman said, speaking to Moses. "May I sit down?"

"Sure," he said, handing her into a chair. "What's your story?"

She was twenty, he supposed, a small, finely put together woman with reddish hair and green eyes and a scatter of freckles across her nose.

"Now why do you want to get to Benson, or Camp Bowie or Tucson?"

"Camp Bowie," she said. "I'm going to get married."

There was a ruckus on the walk, men yelling and swearing, then the Ketchel boys rode their horses back and forth in front of the door, alarming patrons. As the

27

clerk ran out, they seized him and dragged him down the street, yelling and pleading for someone to help him.

"High spirits," Moses said dryly. Then he slapped his hand on the table and said, "I've had about enough of this myself. 'Scuse me."

He got up and hurried outside, pushing his way through the crowd jamming the doorway. Jim Ketchel had let go of the clerk, but Pete still had him by the wrist and was dragging him up and down the street, in constant danger of being kicked badly by the horse.

Joe Moses yelled, "Let him go, Pete!"

Ketchel stopped and looked around; he still hung on to the clerk who sobbed and tried to pull his torn clothing together. Then he saw Moses and grinned. "You're spoiling my fun, Joe."

"And you've spoiled my evening," Moses said. "Let him go."

The crowd fell silent as Jim Ketchel roweled his horse over and looked down at Moses. "Now, we don't want any trouble. Just a little fun."

"You've had nothing but fun since you hit town. Time to go now."

Jim Ketchel stared. "You runnin' us out, Joe?" He turned around and looked at his brother, twenty feet away. "Hey, you hear that, Pete? What do you say we —"

That was as far as he got for Moses grabbed Ketchel's horse high on the neck and swung up, Indian style, letting the horse lift him as he reared. Then he kicked out with both feet and drove Jim Ketchel from the saddle. He went off the back of the horse and hit the street solidly.

Moses was in the saddle and he handled the horse with his knees, wheeling him around, driving him toward Pete Ketchel. He went at him like a gunboat ramming a picket ship, and both horses went down. Moses jumped clear and was out of it, standing to one side, when the dust began to thin.

Jim Ketchel was sitting in the dust, swearing and holding his wrenched leg; Pete slowly got to his feet, shaking his head as though wondering what had happened.

Moses said, "I got trouble for you, Pete, if you want it."

Ketchel got up. He had lost his portside pistol and the other was pushed around to the back of his hip. He took off his hat and flogged rank clouds of dust from his clothes. "God damn it," he said, "we was just lettin' off steam."

"So was I," Moses commented. "Let's

have a quiet night, huh?"

"Ah, hell — all right, Joe. All right." He retrieved his lost pistol and straightened himself a little as Joe Moses turned and went back into the hotel.

A man standing near the door smiled and took the cigar from his mouth. "You want to be marshal of this town, Sergeant?"

"You couldn't give me this town," Moses told him.

There was a man at his table, and the young woman. The man wore a smile on his melon face and showed the gold caps on his teeth. "Well done, Sergeant. I'll see that your commanding officer hears of this."

"Who are you?" Moses asked, sitting down.

"Franklin Erskine, Sergeant. Indian agent, newly assigned to the San Carlos reservation. I'll be ready to leave in the morning."

"Then you'll leave by yourself," Moses said frankly. "I already have a passenger. Two in fact." He looked at the young woman. "What's your name?"

"Nora Frazer."

"Now see here," Erskine said, but stopped when Moses looked at him.

"You interrupted the lady," he said

30

mildly. He gave his attention and his smile to Nora Frazer. "Which officer —"

"Lieutenant Malcolm Baker, Sergeant. Do you know him?"

"Yes, well," Moses said. "Six o'clock and I won't wait."

She smiled. "I didn't think you were the kind that would."

"As a representative of the United States Bureau of Indian Affairs —"

"There'll be a military escort through in a few weeks," Moses said, interrupting him. "They may even have an ambulance for you to ride in. I'll report that you're here, sir. So why don't you enjoy the delights of Lordsburg?"

"Delights?" Erskine reared back and his chair groaned under the sudden shift of weight. "You're mad, Sergeant. Shooting in the streets. Yelling half the night. Fights." He blew out a breath. "If there was a telegraph in operation I'd wire for reassignment." He pushed away from the table and got up, clapping his hat on solidly. "And I don't like your manner, Sergeant. Don't like it at all. Your commanding officer will receive my report. Rest assured of it."

He stalked out and Moses leaned his head in his hand and idly scratched the back of his head. "Now you know why we have Indian trouble," he said.

Nora Frazer was studying him carefully. She said, "You're irritated, even half angry, to be saddled with a woman on the trip, aren't you?"

"Two women," he said. "Captain Dane's wife is going too."

"Is there room for three in the buggy?"

"It'll be crowded, but it'll be something we have to put up with," he said. Then he tipped his head back and laughed. "I'll be honest with you, Miss Frazer. I'm taking you because I figure if I don't, you'll be after me next trip. Besides, you might as well go together. I don't think I could put up with scared women twice."

"We'll try not to be a bother, Sergeant," she said stiffly.

"You will be," he assured her.

"How brave you are in your duty," she snapped, getting up. "And how stupidly smug."

He watched her flounce out, her step angry, then he laughed and poured the last of his cold coffee.

2

Dawn was a bare blush when Sergeant Joe Moses went to the stable and hitched his buggy and the street was quiet when he drove to the express office and stopped. Curly Jensen, the agent, was walking along, yawning and running his fingers through his uncombed hair; he fitted his key to the door and opened it, saying, "Couldn't you start an hour later?"

"Sunup is sunup," Moses said.

Jensen went behind the counter and put his hand on the dial of the safe. "You want to turn your back, Joe? Company rules." He worked the combination, opened the heavy door and put a small metal box on the counter. "You can turn back now. The paymasters at Bowie and Camp Lowell have keys for this."

Moses lifted the box; it was not at all heavy. "Paper money. Well, I guess it spends the same as specie. What else?"

"Mail," Jensen said, tossing a sack on the counter. "Military dispatches." He slapped a fat leather case beside the sack. Then he smiled. "Hear you're taking the women along." He winked. "An officer's wife and an officer's wife-to-be. You bucking for a promotion, Joe?"

"You never can tell," Moses said and took everything out to the buggy and locked it in the metal box under the seat. When he looked around he saw Bill Kelly at the far end of the street, dressed in riding clothes and standing by his horse.

Jensen came out, saw Kelly and frowned. "He must want to get to Tucson pretty bad."

"Seems like it," Moses said. "He been in town long?"

"Came in on the last stage," Jensen said.

Moses was getting into the buggy and he stopped. "With the payroll?"

"Well, yes," Jensen said. Then he shook his head and laughed. "Aw come on, Joe. Do you have to suspect everybody of something?"

"Until I know better," Moses admitted and got into the rig. He buckled on his pistol belt and placed the shotguns, muzzles down, through the leather straps riveted to the dashboard and drove on to the hotel. His pocket watch said a quarter to six and he had hardly pulled up at the door when Mrs. Dane and Nora Frazer came out, baggage in hand.

He got down and strapped it in behind the seat, handed them up, then got in and drove out of town, water bags sloshing. The road cut across the desert, rising gradually to the mountains beyond.

The dust boiled up around the buggy and Moses pulled his neckerchief over his nose and the women used scarves. It was a tight pinch, three on a seat, and he knew it would get a lot more uncomfortable before the journey ended.

At mid-morning he looked back and saw that Kelly was a mile behind them, riding along, taking his time and probably telling himself that this was going to be an easy way to get through. The first two days wouldn't be bad; but after that they'd be in Cochise's back yard and then Kelly would have to watch himself pretty close.

When Moses arrived at Abe Wichles' station shortly before noon, the temperature stood at over a hundred with the promise of going higher before the sun went down. He got down and helped the ladies, then opened his express box and handed Wichles some rolled magazines.

The old man took them and grinned his thanks, then watched Bill Kelly approach the station. One of the hostlers took the buggy to the shade trees and the ladies walked over and stood by the watering trough, wilting in silence. Then Nora Frazer took her handkerchief and wet it and washed the dust from her face.

Kelly came into the yard, swung down and knocked dust from his clothes with his hat. As Moses watched him out of the corner of his eye, he saw two men step out of the station door. In that brief glimpse he recognized Jim and Pete Ketchel.

Then Kelly said, "Where is it?" Joe Moses knew what he meant and knew why the Ketchel boys had made a night ride of it. He reached for his pistols as Kelly drew his and the two Ketchel boys jumped in opposite directions.

Kelly fired first. Joe Moses figured he would and he went rolling down into the dirt, Kelly's bullet missing him by five inches.

The Ketchel boys had their guns out but hadn't fired and Kelly was yelling, "Shoot, damn you!"

Moses stopped rolling and lay prone, both elbows braced. He fired and Kelly staggered back, surprise on his face. His eyes got round and his mouth dropped open as though he were going to say something and didn't know quite what; then his knees bent, he dropped his pistols and fell on his face, raising a bomb of dust.

Moses turned to the Ketchel boys. Jim was standing there with his hands in the air and Pete didn't look like a man who was going to shoot anybody. Slowly Moses got up and holstered one of his pistols, refastening the flap carefully. Then he walked over to them and said, "Now, you tell me about it and no damned lies."

Pete Ketchel swallowed. "Kelly said all we had to do was to step out when he signaled with his hat. Ain't that right, Jim?"

The man nodded. "There wasn't any shootin' called for, Joe. We was just goin' to look like we had him backed up." He looked at Bill Kelly. "He was goin' to take care of everything, Joe."

"You want the money that bad?" Moses asked. He broke open his .44 and replaced the spent cartridge. "There's no marshal in Lordsburg for me to fetch. None this side of Tucson. And I'm not going to take you there to turn you in. But I am goin' to make a report of this, so I figure you've got a six-day head start. Don't waste it."

Jim nodded and Pete nodded. "Our mine's petered out," Pete said. "Five hundred looked good to us, Joe. Can you understand that?"

"Yes," Moses said frankly. "Now get

your horses and water bags filled and get goin'. That's more of a chance than I thought I had." He holstered his pistol, flapped it and turned back to where Abe Wichles stood. "Don't you have sense enough to duck, Abe?"

"They wasn't shootin' at me," Wichles said, staring at the dead man. "I guess we'd better get him in the ground. He'll get pretty ripe in this heat. Did he have a name that you recall?"

"Bill Kelly, if you want to put up a head-board."

Wichles nodded. "Died of gunshot."

"And greed," Moses added and walked over to the shade. Sweat ran down his face as he took off his hat and splashed water over his head. He didn't bother to dry himself; the heat would evaporate it in a moment. The women were watching him, not saying anything, but he could tell by their frozen expressions that they were shocked.

"He wanted the payroll," Moses said. "Nearly twenty thousand dollars under the seat." He motioned toward the station. "Fifteen minutes to eat, and I suggest you do because it'll be the last cooked meal or coffee until we reach Bowie."

Mrs. Dane said, "He seemed like such a nice man."

"Things ain't always what they seem," Moses told her. "Better come inside, ladies."

He went on ahead and got some coffee and took it to the bar. The room was not large and the bar was two planks erected along one wall. When the women came in and sat down, a Mexican brought their food and some coffee. Wichles came in and put his magazines on the bar. He poured a drink of whiskey for himself and downed it, then leaned heavily on the bar.

"You ladies must be in some rush to get to Tucson," Wichles said. "Mighty uncomfortable, that buggy. Mighty dangerous too."

Moses said, "Mind your own business, Abe."

"Now, that's hard for a fella my age. Means breakin' a lifelong habit." He sighed and wiped his hand across his face. "I do wish I had a trade, Joe. Wouldn't be here if I had."

One of the Mexicans came in, hat in hand. "Señor Weekles, where you want heem buried?"

"Well, far enough away so he don't pollute the well," Wichles said. "And deep, you hear. I don't want varmints diggin' him up." He shook his head. "Got to tell 'em everything. Can't figure a thing out for themselves."

Nora Frazer abruptly got up from the table and went outside.

Wichles followed her with his eyes, then said, "What ails her?"

Moses said nothing; he went out and found Nora Frazer standing by the buggy. Her back was to him and he saw her hands near her face and knew that she was crying. He took a cigar from his pocket, lit it and said, "One of the hardest things to learn out here is that nothing is going to be like it was back home."

She turned and let him see her red eyes. "I am crying, Sergeant, because no one cares a whit for that poor man."

"Yes,'m, that's right. Nobody cares. He wasn't worth carin' about."

"How can you make that decision? What right have you?"

"I guess because there's no one else to make it," he said. "Kelly took me for a greenhorn fool. I carry the army payroll just about every two months. He's not the first man who wanted that money. Only this time it wasn't gold and silver. It's paper money, which makes it a lot easier to steal." He sighed and looked at the ash on his cigar.

"You knew that he was going to rob you? You were sure of that?"

"Yes," Moses said. "It was in his eyes when he rode into the yard. There wasn't a doubt in my mind. You heard him ask for it. He made his mistake when he thought it would be easy."

"I suppose you're right," Nora Frazer said. "But it's hard to understand, happening so quickly, and so finally. No chance to mend anything. No chance to back away and admit it was a mistake." She reached out and put her hand on his arm. "What is Camp Bowie like?"

"Trees, good water. Fair quarters. You'll be comfortable there. But it'll also be dull for you. All you'll see is the post."

"I don't think I'll mind that," she said. "Are there other wives —"

"Three," Moses said. "I suppose you'll get married right away?"

"Why of course," Nora said. "That was a silly question, Sergeant." She looked at him and he kept watching her and this made her a little nervous. "Sergeant, it's all planned."

"Nothing's planned," Moses said gently. "Don't fool yourself."

Her face took on a deep color, as though she had just stepped out of a hot bath. "Are you calling me a liar?"

"I'm asking you to stick to the truth,"

Moses said. "Especially with yourself. I carry the mail. Lieutenant Baker hasn't answered your letters for nearly five months. And every trip through I carry two or three from you."

"Well, he's not much for writing! Is that so odd?"

"Last year he wrote regularly," Moses said.

"Well, if you knew so much, why did you offer to take me with you in the first place?".

"Because you have a right to hand him back his ring and go home and marry someone else," Moses said frankly.

"Sergeant, I think when I tell Mr. Baker that he'll be very upset about it. You *are* in the army, you know. I think you forget that."

"Not for one minute day or night," Moses assured her. "I chose the army. Quit high school after my second year to join. You tell Lieutenant Baker what I said. If you don't, I will." He turned and leaned against the wheel of the buggy and studied her. "I could have easily told you no in Lordsburg. I could have sent you back home with that one word, or at least made you wait three weeks for a military detail to come through. But I didn't want to do that. You've waited too long. Isn't that right?"

She nodded and looked down. "I've waited a very long time, Sergeant. And it hasn't been easy." Then she raised her eyes. "Do you have an answer for me, Sergeant?"

"About Mr. Baker?" He shook his head. "I don't answer for another man. But there's no other woman that I know of, if that eases your mind."

"Thank you," she said softly. "I sincerely mean that."

"It's time to go," he said and handed her into the rig. Then he went into the station to get Mildred Dane.

Wichles came out and checked the harness. The team was fresh and frisky and he said, "Bring me some canned things from Tucson."

"What do you want?"

"Oh, peaches, if any came in on the steamer to Yuma. And be careful."

"I try," Moses said and clucked the team into motion.

He left the yard and walked the horses up along the climbing slash, toward the summit. He'd be there by nightfall. The heat was intense, there was no breeze at all and the desert bounced the sun back at them. It felt as though they were driving

43

across the top of a huge cookstove.

Mildred Dane was quiet and Nora Frazer had her own thoughts. Joe Moses let the silence run for a time, then broke it. "A few things we've got to understand, ladies. Once we reach the summit we're in Apache country. Each camp will be cold — no light, no fires. And no talk. Not even whispering. We'll rest two hours and move three or four times during the night."

"Whatever you say, Sergeant," Mrs. Dane said. "I'm most confident that you know what you're doing and what's best for us."

"Thank you, ma'am. But I want to point out that it won't be an easy time."

"We understand," she said, "and we'll be no trouble to you."

"It occurred to me that you could take turns sleeping in the buggy. The box is small, but you could curl up there and there's no danger of waking up with a rattlesnake in your blankets."

"Rattlesnake?" Nora said quickly.

"Well, it can happen," Moses said. He pointed ahead to the summit. "Once we start through the pass the game begins."

"Game?" Mrs. Dane said.

"Yes'm. The Apaches try to get me and I try to keep 'em from gettin' me. We'll be watched every step of the way. At night, they'll stop when we stop. They're none too happy about the idea of jumpin' me at night unless they think they'll get me first crack. That's why we make no noise. They've got ears sharp enough to hear a lizard mess on a rock, so they'll listen for any sound we make; and once they know exactly where we are they'll come in on their bellies with knives. So if you hear a rattlesnake buzz, figure it's an Apache tryin' to get you to jump up or scream. You understand what I'm talkin' about, ladies? We only get one mistake."

They thought about this awhile, then Nora Frazer said, "Sergeant, if one of us did something, I mean —"

"They'd go for me," Moses said. "A woman is no good to 'em dead."

"Thank you for your honesty," Mildred Dane said. "We'll try hard not to make a mistake."

"Won't they hear the buggy when we move from place to place?" Nora asked.

Moses nodded. "But they won't jump the rig. Too risky. They'd have to get me the first second before I let the horses run and started using my shotguns. The dangerous time is when we stop to rest." Then he turned and looked at them and smiled.

"Now you ladies don't fret about this. We'll take it a mile at a time and when the sun comes up you'll be in Camp Bowie enjoying a bath. I stop an hour there."

"An hour?" they said together. Then Mrs. Dane said, "Sergeant, your generosity almost overwhelms me at times. It really does."

The trail seemed to grow steeper as they approached the mountains, and the setting sun cast long, deep shadows. Every fissure stood out bold and threatening, a dark hiding place for many dangers. Dusk found them in the pass, overpowered by the sheer walls and lofty reaches, and the horses set up an echoing racket as they moved along. Sergeant Moses collapsed the top of the buggy so he could look up and study the rimrock; he seemed to see nothing to alarm him, yet he rode with caution, a shotgun in his hands.

Darkness, full, blanketing, did not stop him; he let the horses walk, guiding themselves, picking their way along a road they knew well. The night was clear and the stars were there, brilliant, by the millions, and they seemed very near. Although the rocks threw off heat, the temperature was dropping and in two hours a man would be

46

hunting his coat to put on.

There was really no road through the pass, but travelers had stopped and cleared away most of the big rocks, which made it somewhat level and smooth; the buggy springs did the rest, making the ride nearly tolerable. The thousand years of rains washing minute particles of rock off the walls had laid a bed of fine sand through the pass. The buggy wheels churned up this dust and it hung around them and behind them so anyone following them would have no trouble; it was a scent that would linger for a half hour, like a man walking through a tomato patch.

When they reached the summit and started down the other side, Joe Moses did not stop. Somewhere in his mind he kept track of the passage of the miles and of the time; and they finally left the high reaches of the pass and began to travel through rocky, brushy land full of deep draws and small canyons.

Finally he stopped the buggy, got down and went around to help the women to the ground. Mildred Dane stifled a groan when her feet touched and he held her, supported her for a moment, then let her go; he could barely make out her smile. Taking both the shotguns, he led them away from the road, a distance of twenty yards, to some scrub timber and motioned for them to sit on the ground.

He passed the canteen around and drank when they were through. There was a slight noise in the rocks across the road and the women became instantly alert; Nora Frazer started to get up, but Joe Moses quickly shook his head and she relaxed.

They remained there for five minutes, making no sound, then the horses snorted and one made a pawing sound with his forefoot. Joe Moses opened his mouth and breathed silently, straining to hear, then he bent and whispered directly into Mildred Dane's ear.

"Carefully, on your hands and knees, go back to the buggy. No sound. Feel your way."

She nodded, indicating that she understood him, and he whispered the same to Nora Frazer. They inched away on all fours, and he watched them and knew that, crouched down like that, the night hid them.

He waited a moment, then carefully pushed the barrel of one shotgun through his belt and held the other in one hand like a double-barreled pistol. The canteen was on the ground and he picked it up and sloshed it around; the sound of the water seemed loud in the stillness. The horses were snorting and turning restlessly now and Moses decided that if he was going to do anything, he'd better do it now.

Carelessly he let the canteen strike against a rock, making the water slosh again; then he heard what he had been listening for — the sound of a callused bare foot whispering on stone. He turned and saw the vague, dark shape of the Apache and he raised the muzzle of the shotgun and fired from the hip.

The muzzle flash would have been blinding if he had not closed his eyes as he pulled the trigger. The Apache fell, flung by the heavy charge; then the silence was broken by a yell. Moses made a jump to one side, turning to face the Apache who raced from his cover in the scrub timber.

Ten yards separated them as he let the Apache have the shotgun blast, watched him stopped and driven down. Then he took the other shotgun from his belt and laid the empty one on the ground.

For fifteen seconds he stood there, waiting, then picked up the empty shotgun and the canteen and walked to the buggy, not caring whether his boots made any noise or not. He hung the canteen, broke open his empty shotgun and fed two brass cartridges into the chambers, then clacked it shut.

"You ladies about ready to continue on?" he asked. "Maybe we can sing some songs to pass the time."

They stood there, staring at him, not talking because he had told them not to. Then he laughed. "It's all right now, ladies; talk if you like."

Nora Frazer asked, "Are they — dead?"

"Yes'm, very dead," Moses told her.

"I don't understand this, Sergeant," Mildred Dane said. "Has the danger passed?"

"Well, for the rest of the night anyway," he said. "Can I help you ladies aboard? I'd like to move on 'cause the smell of those Apaches is making the horses mighty nervous."

"Whatever you say, Sergeant," Mrs. Dane said and got into the rig. He helped Nora Frazer to the seat, got in and drove on.

"Just so as you'll have the straight of it," Moses said, "I'll take you step by step through what happened. I figured the Apaches had their look at you two ladies sometime before dark, and I figured that maybe a couple of bucks thought you'd make good wives and would have a try."

"What a horrible thought," Nora Frazer said.

"Maybe, but they still had that notion. Anyway, when I stopped, we all got out and moved away from the buggy. That was to give the Apaches a chance to look it over. When they found us gone, they knew we were in the rocks on the other side of the road or the scrub timber. I gave 'em a chance to nose around, then sent you back to the rig on your hands and knees, knowin' they wouldn't look there again. All I had to do then was wait until the horses told me the Apaches were close. You see, I've trained all these horses to hate Apaches. Got me an old Apache to whip the horses every day. They get one whiff of an Apache and they get nervous and let me know about it."

"I heard you make a noise," Mrs. Dane said. "You forced them to jump you."

"Sure. It's easier when you know they're coming," Moses said.

"The shotgun blast blinded me," Nora said, "I don't see how . . ."

He laughed. "Since I know when I'm going to shoot, I aim and close my eyes for a second. That way I'm not blinded." He took out his tobacco and rolled a cigarette then nonchalantly struck a match. "So I figure we're going to make it the rest of the way to Bowie with no trouble at all. You

51

see, those two bucks figured they'd make a little brag, kill me, take you back for wives, and be big men with Cochise. But they're dead and right now six or eight Apaches are standing around that clearing and talking about how they should get the hell out of there because it's a night full of bad medicine."

"If you think that, Sergeant," Mrs. Dane said, "then I believe it. And you speak excellent French."

"I do?"

"Yes, that part about getting the hell out was excellently done."

He turned his head and stared at her for a moment, then laughed. "Do you know *Tenting Tonight?*"

"Very well," Mildred Dane said.

"Then suppose you sing the melody and I'll do the harmony."

"In addition to your other talents, you have an ear for music too?"

"Hit your pitch and let's go," Moses said.

"I think you're both completely mad," Nora Frazer said and acted as though she were going to cry.

"My dear," Mildred Dane said, "you have to give with things. Try and you'll feel better." Then she sang a few bars of the song in a rich alto voice. "That about right, Sergeant?"

"Why, that's just dandy," Moses said and sang the harmony.

Camp Bowie, in the sun's first bright flush, was not particularly attractive: a clutter of buildings, some trees and a good spring, and a sentry standing duty at the pole archway. He called the corporal of the guard as soon as he saw Joe Moses' buggy approaching, and by the time Moses passed through and drove across the dusty parade ground, a cluster of enlisted men had gathered near headquarters and the officer of the day had come out.

Moses saluted and said, "Will you tell Mr. Baker I've arrived, sir?"

Lieutenant Jefferson Travis removed his campaign hat and scratched his head. "That's going to be difficult, Sergeant. Lieutenant Baker went to Tucson two days ago. Permanent change of post." He stepped down off the porch and went to the buggy and helped the women down. "My wife will make you comfortable until I can have quarters cleaned." He turned to an enlisted man and motioned him over.

"I'm afraid we'll have to leave with Sergeant Moses," Mrs. Dane said. "My husband's at Lowell and now that Lieutenant Baker is gone —" She shrugged. "Perhaps just a bath, a change of clothes and some coffee."

"Of course," Travis said. "Corporal, take the ladies' bags." He touched his hat with his forefinger and walked back to the porch where Moses waited. "Come inside, Sergeant." He put his arm around Moses' shoulders, then as he stepped through the door he glanced back to see if he was out of earshot. The women were walking across the parade ground toward the quarters and Travis said, "Moses, what the hell's the idea of bringing these women with you?"

"They wanted to come along," he said and slumped into a chair. Then he reached across the desk and helped himself to one of Travis' cigars and a match. He told Lieutenant Travis about Bill Kelly and the shooting at Abe Wichles' station, and the little trouble he had had just this side of the pass.

"The money is still in the strongbox?" Travis asked.

"Yes, sir. It's safe there. No one knows it's there." He puffed on the cigar and closed his eyes. "Mrs. Dane's quite a woman. Someone ought to knock some sense into the captain."

Jefferson Travis shook his head.

"Thanks, no. And you're not doing her any favor, Joe. You know that?"

"What I don't know would fill a library," Moses admitted. "But I figure when a man brings his sons on an army post and they live with him and not their mother, then something's wrong. Then I meet Mrs. Dane and I know damned good and well she's waited long enough. Dane doesn't know she's coming out here; I'm sure of that. He'd have had an escort for her if he'd known."

"Or if he'd wanted her out here," Travis said. "He doesn't want her, Joe. That's been plain enough to me for some time. He lives for those two boys."

"Yeah, that's a fact. So I've got a long nose."

"And the other woman?" Travis asked. "Baker's changed his mind. You know it and I know it. She's come a long way for a broken heart."

"Maybe she'll slap Baker's face," Moses suggested. "I'd enjoy that."

"Now, that's not a nice way to talk about your superior officer," Travis said, suppressing a grin.

Joe Moses shook his head. "You're my commanding officer, sir, and the only thing that's kept you from belting Mr.

Baker is your wife, who told you you'd sleep in the stables for a week if you did."

"Oh, now, see here, Sergeant —" Then Jefferson Travis laughed and tilted back his chair. "I'll tell you what I'm going to do, Joe. I'm going to let you stew a little in this mess you're stirring up. You've brought a nice young girl here so Baker can tell her she's wasted her time. Now she may turn around and belt you."

Moses shook his head. "She knows how it is. But she hasn't admitted it yet. On my next trip through to Lordsburg I'll be bringing her back, so she can go home and marry a nice guy who'll take care of her." He pushed himself erect. "Any dispatches, sir? I have a few for you."

"Every time I see you it's more paper work," Travis said and walked with Moses to the buggy. The strongbox was unlocked with the OD's key and Travis examined the dispatch case, took what was earmarked for his desk and put the rest back. The OD locked the box and pocketed the key.

"There's a government man in Lordsburg," Moses said. "Name's Franklin Erskine. Indian agent, I guess. I told him to wait for a detail coming through. His nose is a little out of joint."

56

Travis blew out a breath and rolled his eyes. "All right, Sergeant, I may take a platoon through in a week or so."

"I felt sure you would," Moses said. He walked across to Travis' quarters and knocked on the door.

Cora Travis opened it, then put her hand lightly against his chest. "Uh-huh, Sergeant. Ladies are bathing."

"I have nothing against ladies bathing," Moses said pleasantly.

"But you're not to watch," she said and came out, closing the door.

"I've just been talking to your husband. An excellent officer, ma'am."

"And there's no use talking like that. You're not going to sell me anything today. Do you understand? Nothing."

Moses got a pained look on his young face. "Why would I want to do a thing like that, ma'am?" He shook his head as though he were having a hard time getting over this dig. "All I came to say was that I bought you a bottle of cooking sherry in Lordsburg. I've got it wrapped in a blanket and —"

"Why," she said, smiling, "that was very thoughtful, Sergeant. Very thoughtful indeed." She started to step off the porch, then stopped. "Now wait a minute. No strings?"

"Oh, none," Moses assured her.

"Are you sure, Sergeant?"

"Well — yes, I guess so."

She looked at him and nodded and smiled; she was young, in her late twenties, pretty in a dark-haired way. Her skin was clear but deeply tanned so that she seemed Spanish. Yet her eyes were blue. "All right, Sergeant, out with it. What does the cooking sherry cost me?"

"Your husband, being the clear thinker that he is, pointed out to me that I may be putting Captain Dane and Mr. Baker in an uncomfortable spot, springing their women on them suddenly, so to speak. So I wondered if they could stay here with you until I told Captain Dane and Mr. Baker and —"

"No," Cora Travis said.

He looked at her. "What do you mean, no?"

"NO, no," she said. "An adverb, meaning a negative vote or decision. A reply of denial or refusal." She reached out and tapped him on the chest with her forefinger. "Joseph A. Moses, you have a habit of doing the things you shouldn't, and it's about time a few things caught up with you. You knew better than to bring them this far, yet you did it. Now, I'm not going to pay off your second thoughts on the matter. Finish what you started."

"Right now it doesn't seem that I should," he said gravely. He took off his hat and ran his fingers through his hair. "You won't change your mind?"

"No, and don't ask me what that means."

He grinned. "If Dane gets mad enough he may hit me with the book of regulations." He turned away, then turned back. "Why do I stick my nose in where it doesn't belong all the time?"

"Because you can't help it," Cora Travis said.

He thought about it, nodded and put his hat back on. "Come on and I'll give you your cooking sherry."

Through the shimmering heat of that day they traveled across the broad, desert floor of a valley with buttes rising monument-like in the distance, while ahead, and turning to shades of purple and blue in the fading sunlight, lay another range of mountains.

That evening they camped in the open and he gathered brush and built a fire and made some coffee. Finally Mrs. Dane said, "Sergeant, won't the Indians see the fire?"

"I guess they're watching us right now," he said matter-of-factly. "But they've been watchin' us all along. The thing is, Apaches are proud. They'd come just so far on their bellies, then they'd yell and rush. In the open this way, they'd have to cover maybe thirty or forty yards in the clear and they know they'd never make it." He lifted his shotgun. "You notice that I never put this thing down? And my spare is never more'n two jumps away. They see that and it holds them back." He smiled. "We'll get some sleep tonight. It just ain't restful, dozin' in the buggy." The coffee started to boil and he pulled it away from the fire. Nora Frazer brought some cups and he poured. Then he squatted and looked from one to the other. "We've got to be smarter than the Apaches, so I figure that one can stretch out and sleep for a spell while the other sits up with me. Then we'll change off. I'll sleep sittin' but the Apaches won't know it. As long as they think I'm halfway alert, they'll keep their distance."

Nora Frazer said, "Sergeant, how can we — leave the camp?"

He scratched the back of his head. "Problem there all right. But I guess you could go to the buggy. No farther though."

They both turned their heads and looked and measured the distance with their eyes, ten yards on the outside. Mildred Dane said, "That seems a most immodest distance, Sergeant."

"Yes'm."

"We'll make the best of it then," Mrs. Dane said and drank her coffee.

They were, Joe Moses thought, a pair of real troopers. The heat had been vicious, the dust a gall and a constant irritation, and the flies in the late afternoon had been particularly hungry; yet he heard no moaning, no complaints from either of them. They were bone-tired and there was no opportunity for a decent rest, but they didn't complain about that either.

He told Nora Frazer to spread her blanket and she curled up near the fire and went to sleep almost immediately. The night was dark and moonless, yet the sky was clear and the stars were winking.

Moses sat away from the fire, one shotgun across his lap and the other by his side. Mildred Dane sat nearby, her arms wrapped around her knees, and for a time neither of them spoke. Moses smoked a cigarette and kept listening to small sounds of animals moving about, hunting.

When Mildred Dane spoke, she did so in the softest of voices. "Do you see my husband often, Sergeant?"

"Yes'm, every time I'm at Lowell. Most every trip." He raised his head and looked at her. "I see the boys too, ma'am. Little Tad's tall for six. Richard's taken to wearin' long pants."

She stared at him a moment as though surprised, then she said, "Thank you. It's been two years since I've seen them, you know. That's a long time for a woman's heart to —"

He waited for her to go on and knew she wouldn't. He took a final puff on his cigarette and ground the butt into the sandy ground. "Ma'am, I probably know more about everybody's business than anyone in the Third Cavalry. Lieutenant Travis says that's because I stick my nose in everybody's business, and maybe he's right there. Nevertheless, there's not much that goes on that I don't know about. Like you and your husband, ma'am. I know he took the boys away from you and that you haven't heard from him for nearly two years. Now I'm not trying to pump you, but you sure ought to know by this time that I'm trying to help you. Else I would have left you in Lordsburg."

"And you think you can help me further, Sergeant?"

Moses shrugged. "I'm not the dumbest guy in the company. Yes, I'd try."

"You know my husband is a very ambitious man," she said. "He's from a good family with a strong tradition of military service behind him." She clasped her hands together and kneaded her fingers. "I married Captain Dane when I was young, not quite eighteen. Everyone thought I was very lucky. I'm twenty-nine now, Sergeant, and I don't think I'm so lucky. I haven't a husband and I've lost my sons. Now there isn't much left, is there?"

"What do you want? Your boys? Or your husband too?"

"I want to save what I can," Mildred Dane said.

"You'll have to make some compromises," Moses told her.

"I'm ready to make them, Sergeant."

A coyote howled loudly and Nora Frazer sat bolt upright. Joe Moses said, "Go back to sleep. It's only a coyote."

"How do you know?" she asked fearfully.

"I know," Moses said and she eased back and pulled the blanket about her.

A moment later Mildred Dane said, "She has a lot of faith in you." Then she looked at him. "I think it's a shame that she has to be hurt."

"It's a shame any of us have to be hurt," Moses said. "But what can you do?"

"You could be there. Help her, if you would."

He shook his head. "I can't go that far. You know how the army is." He pointed to the hooks on his sleeve. "There's a long way between a lieutenant and a sergeant." He shook his head again. "I can only do what I've already done and bring her through to Camp Lowell. The rest — well, it'll just be some crying and facing up to the facts. Women get some pretty foolish

64

notions about there just being one man in the world."

"Don't men think there's only one woman?"

"I never knew one that did. Known a lot who thought it was too much trouble to change, but one who really thought so — no." He smiled. "Get some sleep."

"And you?"

"I'll doze. It's the best I ever do on this kind of duty."

They reached Tucson and then Camp Lowell in the morning of the fourth day and drove through the main gate with the corporal of the guard yelling for the sergeant and the sergeant bellowing for the officer of the day, who came out of the guardhouse on the double.

Moses skirted the parade and stopped near the guardhouse as the officer of the day hurried up to hand the ladies down. "Mr. Caslin," Moses said, "may I present Captain Dane's wife, and Miss Nora Frazer, Mr. Baker's betrothed."

"Betrothed?" Caslin said, his mouth slack. "Oh, of course. My honor, ladies. Won't you step to the shade? The sun's beastly hot." He snapped his fingers. "Corporal, tend to their luggage." He motioned for the sergeant of the guard to come up. "My compliments to Captain Dane and Mr. Baker, but inform them —"

"Captain Dane's off the post, sir."

"Well, then, tell Mr. Baker —"

"Yes, sir." The sergeant saluted and dashed toward headquarters and Lieutenant Caslin produced a key from his pocket and unlocked the metal box under the seat.

Moses stepped to the porch and stood near Mrs. Dane and Nora Frazer. He studied them from the tail of his eye: they stood tense and nervous and tried not to. He said, "Excuse me, ladies," and left the porch. Caslin was turning the money over to the guards who took it into his office to wait for the paymaster. The mail was given to a headquarters orderly. "Mr. Caslin, sir, I suggest that the ladies be taken to quarters and allowed to freshen up before —"

"Yes, of course, Sergeant. Stupid of me." He went to them. "Ladies, if you'll come with me, I'll show you to quarters."

They went with him, but not before Mildred Dane looked back and thanked Moses with a smile. When they were out of earshot, Moses got in the buggy and drove to the stables where he unhitched the horses and turned them into the corral, then pushed the buggy inside the farrier sergeant's building. He locked his weapons in the metal strongbox, then walked wearily toward the barracks area a hundred yards away.

He shared quarters with three other sergeants, but they were on duty; so he filled the wooden tub with water, bathed, changed his clothes, then stretched out on his bunk and slept for six hours. He heard through the haze of sleep a few bugle calls, then someone came into the room and shook him. Moses opened one eye and recognized a headquarters orderly.

"The old man wants to see you, Joe."

"All right," Moses said and got up. He straightened his uniform, put on his kepi, and left the barracks. Headquarters was aslant across the parade and, although regulations forbid it, he cut straight across. Two orderlies passed him through the outer and inner offices, then he knocked on the commanding officer's door and went in.

Major Fickland dispensed with the salute and waved Moses into a chair, then said, "Of course you wouldn't have a chance to see the Tucson paper, so I can't blame you for that. But you've got us in a hell of a pickle here, Moses, bringing Mrs.

Dane on the post." He picked up a newspaper and tossed it in Moses' lap. "Second page, third column, about halfway down."

Moses searched for it, found it, read it to himself, then read it aloud. "Señor Miguel Alvarez, distinguished Tucson merchant, announces the engagement of his daughter, Doña Luisa Alvarez to Captain George Dane —" He looked up. "Hell, the man's got one wife already!"

Major Fickland shook his head. "Over a month ago a Tucson attorney filed papers and they were mailed to her, through Yuma, to San Francisco, and then by train to the east. She must have left before they got there. Moses, Dane's divorcing her." He held up his hand as Moses opened his mouth. "Now damn it, don't start telling me what he can or can't do! And don't tell George Dane that either."

"Yes, sir."

Fickland stroked his mustache. "I have no way of knowing whether Mrs. Dane has seen a paper yet, so I might suggest that you call on her."

"Call, sir?"

"Yes, damn it. Well, after all, you must have gotten to know her on the trip here." He got up and walked around the room, his lean body bent slightly. "Oh, this is going to be sticky business, Sergeant. Very sticky indeed. In my eighteen years of service I've never come up against it — a divorce. Dane's taking a chance with his career, I can tell you that. And if the other woman was less than she is, he'd be through. There's been no breath of anything improper, you understand. She's fond of the boys and —" He stopped and pulled at his lip. "That's another thing. The boys are living in Tucson with the Alvarez family."

"Oh, that's just dandy, sir. Do they call her mother, sir?"

"Now don't get smart, Moses!" He calmed himself, then sat down on the edge of his desk. "You had no way of knowing these things, or did you?"

"Me, sir? I don't stick my nose in an officer's business."

"You don't like Dane," Fickland said. "You've never liked him. Be honest with me, Sergeant."

"He's a piss-poor excuse for an officer, sir. He likes the easy assignments."

"Well," Fickland said, "I asked, didn't I? All right, Joe. I don't have anything more to say." Moses started to get up, then stopped when Fickland spoke. "The young lady — what's her name? —" He snapped his fingers.

"Frazer, sir. Nora Frazer."

"Yes. What the devil do you expect she'll do on this post?"

"She came to marry Mr. Baker, sir."

Fickland snorted. "Now we both know Baker's an utter ass! He's not going to marry her or anyone because he can't make up his mind on any one thing and keep it that way ten minutes." He wiped a hand across his face. "You don't plead innocent on this one, Joe. And don't try it." He held up both hands. "A patrol is going through so I'm giving them ten days on the post. For God's sake *you* keep out of trouble, will you?"

"Well, I always try, Major."

"This time, try harder," Fickland instructed. "Dismissed."

Moses went out and one of the orderlies grinned because the major's voice, when raised to a shout, came through walls very easily.

"I've never heard him in better voice," the orderly said.

"Stick around," Moses advised and went out.

The sun was down and he stood on the porch a moment, then walked across to the mess hall and talked with the cooks awhile. When he left he had two beef sandwiches and a mug of coffee.

He took these to his quarters and sat on his bed and ate. Sergeant Mulligan, who had line duty, came in, took off his cap and hung it up, then flopped on his bunk. He was a twenty-year man who had been up and down the ranks many times. His face was heavy and blocky and scarred because he was too slow to duck and too tough to whip.

"Hear you brought back a couple of packages, bucko," Mulligan said, grinning. "Things may liven up around here."

"Go fight Indians," Moses suggested. "Where's Carter and Raney?" He looked toward the neatly made bunks.

"Patrol. Be back day after tomorrow."

"Well, I won't have to listen to Raney snore tonight anyway," Moses said. He finished off the sandwiches and drank his coffee, then looked up as boots treaded heavily toward his door.

Lieutenant Baker opened the door without knocking and stood there, a tall young man in his early twenties. He had a round, unlined face and large brown eyes and a full, sensuous mouth.

"Sergeant Moses, I want a word with you!" Baker said.

"Well, sir, since you busted in here

without invitation and without knocking, suppose you say what's on your mind."

Mulligan swallowed hard; every time he talked to an officer like that he had a tour of the guardhouse and he was interested in seeing how this was going to turn out.

Baker looked at the Irishman and said, "Get out! This is a private conversation."

"Sit still," Moses said gently. "Mr. Baker knows the regulations. This is our quarters and he's out of line." He looked steadily at Malcolm Baker. "Say what you have to say, sir, then leave us alone."

"Very well," Baker said. "Sergeant, you've caused me a grave inconvenience. I'm not going to pass it off without some satisfaction." He set his mouth into a firm line. "After the evening mess I'd like to see you behind the rifle butts."

"You want to fight, sir?" Moses asked.

"I know what you're thinking," Baker said. "There'll be no rank connected with this, Sergeant. Your friend can bear witness to it. I'll strip to the waist. You'll do the same." He pointed his finger. "I'm going to teach you something, Moses. A lesson well learned, and you will learn it well before I'm through."

"Well," Moses said, "if you've just got to have it that way, I wouldn't want to disappoint you." He studied Baker. "Have you seen Miss Frazer yet?"

"No."

"I would. You might not look too good afterward — sir."

Baker opened his mouth to speak, then closed it and stalked out, slamming the door. Moses eased back on his bunk and Mulligan licked his lips and reached for the water jug. He drank and put it back, then said, "I guess this'll be a private affair between you two."

"You know it has to be."

"You know, it's too bad. Some of the lads would like to see it."

"Let's not figure I've licked him until I've done it," Moses said.

"Why, there's no doubt in me mind but what you'll do it," Mulligan said. "And I'd put me mark on him if I were you." I'd put it on good." He leaned forward and spoke softly. "I can see what the man's thinkin' and I tell you now to forget it. He's bettin' that your years of soldierin' will make you hold back because he's an officer and you know what a man can get for strikin' an officer. And I'm sayin' not to hold back. You hear me, Joe? You give it to him like you would any other man." He settled back on his bunk then, convinced that his logic was beyond debate.

When mess call was blown, Joe Moses got up, put on his kepi and left the barracks, walking down to the company mess. He stood in the sergeants' line and was moving slowly toward the door when an orderly found him. He motioned for him to step out of the line, then said, "Joe, Mrs. Dane asked me to find you. She's in Quarters C."

"Hell, I haven't had my supper," Moses said, then sighed. "All right, Corporal." He took a wistful look at the mess line and sniffed the flavors of beef and hot biscuits, then turned and cut diagonally across the parade. The sun was down and the light was fading as he mounted the wooden walk under the porch overhangs and went past the sutler's store and the bachelor officers' quarters.

Quarters C was on the corner; he knocked and Mildred Dane opened the door then stood back so he could step inside. She had changed to a cotton dress that flattered her good figure and her hair was fixed a little differently; he was struck by the fact that she was really a young, very pretty woman.

"I'm sorry to have taken you away from mess, Sergeant. Won't you sit down?"

"Thank you, ma'am." He put his hat on

a side table and took a chair. The rooms were not large, not even the major's, but they were clean and the furniture was good but very plain, the kind that could endure the wear and tear and hand-me-down from one officer to another.

She said, "Don't you think it's about time we dropped the 'ma'am' and 'sergeant'?"

He thought about it. "You think it's quite proper?"

"Just what is proper anyway?" She sat down across from him and rested her hands in her lap. "Joe, I saw the Tucson paper. Several of the officers' wives came to pay their respects and they happened to 'forget' a copy."

"Opened to that page, of course," Moses said. "The bitches."

"Well, I had to find out," Mildred Dane said. "And really I think they were doing the kind thing. No woman likes to have her composure break in public. At least I could do my crying in private."

"You didn't waste time crying," he said.

"No, I was too angry for that. Joe, will you drive me to Tucson?"

"Now?"

"Will there be a better time?"

He thought of Malcolm Baker, but only briefly. "I'll get a buggy hitched." He got up and turned to the door, then stopped there. "You're sure you want to see him tonight?"

"Yes, very sure."

That settled it in Moses' mind and he went out, walking toward the stable area. He wheeled the buggy out of farrier's shed, got his team and was harnessing them when Lieutenant Malcolm Baker appeared. He stood in the doorway, legs spread, hands on his hips.

"Moses, I waited for you." Then he stepped inside. "But this is as good a place as any."

"No time now," Moses said dryly.

"We're going to take the time," Baker said, stripping off his shirt and tossing it into one of the stalls.

"Better put it where you can remember it afterward," Moses said.

He didn't expect Baker to rush him then, but the man did. It caught Moses by surprise and he barely had time to duck out of the way. Baker crashed into the off-wheel of the buggy, grunted and turned clumsily, then staggered a bit, both hands pressed against his rib cage.

"Are you hurt, sir?" Moses asked. He could see that Baker was hurt, yet it took him a few seconds to figure out what had happened. Baker had rammed into the iron rim of the buggy wheel, taking the brunt of it with the ribs on his left side.

He held himself and gasped for air, his face twisted in pain.

Moses said, "Better let me help you to the infirmary, sir."

"Touch me — and I'll kill you," Baker gasped.

"Why don't you start actin' like a man instead of some snot-nosed kid?" Moses said flatly. "You're mad at me because I brought your girl here, when the truth of the matter is you don't have guts enough to tell her to her face that you're a fickle bastard who just wants to fool around." He reached out to help Baker, who doubled his fist. It pushed anger to the surface of Moses' eyes. "You lay that on me and I'll stomp a hole in your head, sir." Then he took hold of Baker's arm and helped him into the buggy and carefully drove over to the infirmary. He left Baker sitting there and went in and got the surgeon.

He came out, a round, jolly man with a bald head and gold-rimmed glasses. As he helped Baker down, he said, "Well, well, Mr. Baker, what have we been doing with ourself?"

"Mr. Baker fell, sir," Moses said. "In the stable yard."

They went inside and Baker was placed in a chair. The surgeon carefully removed the top half of his underwear, letting it drop around Baker's hips. There was a long, vivid welt across the man's ribs and some swelling, and when the surgeon prodded gently with his fingers, Baker jumped and sucked in his breath sharply.

Moses stood there for a moment, then went out, got into his rig and drove around the parade to Quarters C. Mildred Dane was waiting on the porch, a shawl around her shoulders; he got down and helped her into the buggy. He drove to the main gate and was stopped by the corporal of the guard.

"You got a pass, Moses?"

"Now you know I'm off duty the minute I deliver the mail," Moses said. "You're so dumb, Case, you'll never make sergeant." He clucked to the team and drove on, taking the town road.

Mildred Dane rode in silence and Joe Moses said nothing; he felt the urge to talk to her, but he couldn't think of anything to say that would help her. She was doing a difficult thing and he wondered if he'd have the guts to do it — go where he wasn't wanted and when he got there, face a situation that couldn't be anything but unpleasant.

Tucson at night was a spectacle, a crowded, wide open town with the broad streets crowded with traffic and the saloons doing a holiday business. Moses would have driven on through, but Mildred Dane put her hand on his arm.

"I'd like to go to the hotel, Joe."

He swung in, got down and tied the team, then went inside with her while she registered. The clerk was a little suspicious because she had no luggage, but Joe Moses kept staring at him and the man kept his mouth shut. There was no helping what the man was thinking, but if he showed any of it in his face, Moses had made up his mind to hit him for it.

He took her key and walked with her up the stairs to the second floor and unlocked her door for her, then stood aside.

"Come in a moment," she said and he struck a match, found the lamps, and got them going. She closed the door. "I'm losing my nerve."

"I don't think so," he said. "What do you want me to do?"

"Would you go to her house and tell him I'm here?"

He nodded. "I don't know how long I'll be. Maybe an hour."

"I'll wait," she said. "I don't suppose the

79

boys — no, it's best to leave them out of it. If such a thing is possible." She bit her lip and turned away from him, as though she were ready to cry and didn't want him to see it. "So much of it hurts me, Joe. George taking the boys, and — well, everything seems to hurt."

"I'll go fetch him," Moses said gently.

She looked at him; her eyes were a bit red, but there were no tears. "Please persuade him to come with you."

"Persuade hell," Moses said. "He'll be here."

He went downstairs and passed through the crowded lobby. The clerk came from around his desk and met Moses just before he stepped outside.

"Ah — Sergeant, how long will the lady be using the room?"

"Go up and ask her," Moses suggested. "Wait, ask her husband. I'm goin' to fetch him now." He watched the man's expression; it amused him to see this man almost make a bad mistake and haul clear of it in time. "You see what you almost stepped into, friend?"

Moses went out and untied his team, then walked around to get into his rig. A tall, dark-haired man with a pair of pistols under his coat leaned against the wheel; he smiled at Joe Moses and said, "I saw your rig. The clerk said you were upstairs with a lady."

"The lady is Captain Dane's wife," Moses said.

The man made a pucker of his mouth and brushed his coat aside to get a cigar; lamplight reflected from the badge pinned to his shirt. "Looks like the captain's got one too many women," he said quietly. "You bring her through?"

"Yes, and it ain't done a thing for my popularity. You want to ride along out to the Alvarez place with me, Al?"

"Why not? It's pretty quiet."

Moses stared at him, then glanced up and down the street choked with riders. The saloons were full of men and noise and music and a lot of men kept rounding the far corner, coming and going to the row of adobes on the back street where the prostitutes plied a brisk trade.

"Yeah, real quiet," Moses said and swung into the buggy. Al Roan got in beside him and they drove out of town.

"I'll keep my job and you can keep yours," Roan said. "All right?" He laughed and pushed his hat to the back of his head. He was thirty and he had a reputation and a past he wasn't too proud of and a hope of living it down. "How was the trip through this time?"

"Some trouble," Moses said and told Roan about Bill Kelly's attempt to lift the army payroll. He didn't mention the Ketchel brothers and he wondered why; he didn't owe them anything. Then he thought about it and decided that they'd made a mistake and were entitled to a chance to not make another one. He knew it was tough, a man being down on his luck. A man could do some damned fool things, then live with the regrets a long time.

"A man never really gets into trouble," Roan said, "until he gets too lazy to work for a living. Well, you've saved me some trouble. A flyer came in on Kelly on the last steamer up the Colorado. He was wanted in Texas for robbery. A hundred and fifty dollars reward. You fill me in on the details and I'll see that you get it."

"Now that's a damn poor amount for a man to die for," Moses said.

The Alvarez hacienda was down a short road, a walled plot nestled beneath some large trees. There was a Mexican at the gate; he came out of a sentry hut and held up a lantern.

"Who passes?" he asked, then saw the

marshal and recognized him.

"I'm Sergeant Moses. I want to see Captain Dane."

Al Roan got down. "You go on ahead, Joe. I'll keep this fella company until you get back." He took the Mexican by the arm and pulled him gently aside and Moses drove on to the large, sprawling house.

When he stopped by a broad terrace, a hostler came out and held the team and Moses went to the door and was met by a servant. He gave the woman the message and paced up and down the terrace for ten minutes until he began to grow irritated. He waited a bit longer, then went to the door and opened it. He stood in the middle of a broad inner court and he could hear voices and laughter and the soft musical run of a piano being played.

As he walked across the court, the servant came out of a room farther down and her expression turned to alarm when she saw him. She hurried up. "Señor, please —"

"Did you tell the captain I was here?"

"Sí."

"That's all I wanted to know." He brushed past her and followed the sound of the music and then stopped in the wide entrance to the parlor. Señor Alvarez, a large, gray man, saw him first and stared, and then his wife, who was attracted by his fixed gaze. Captain George Dane was leaning against the piano, his tall body bent while his fiancée played. Then he too sensed an intrusion and looked around and straightened. He was a distinguished looking man with a sweeping mustache and brown wavy hair.

Doña Luisa stopped playing and looked around. George Dane took a step away from the piano and said, "What is the meaning of this intrusion, Sergeant Moses?" He had a full, rich, resonant voice and a way of standing straight and military.

"I asked the servant to —"

"I'm aware of that," Dane said curtly. "Sergeant, if I'd wanted to see you I'd have invited you in. You're being rude to my hosts."

"For that I apologize, sir. However, there's a matter I have to discuss confidentially, sir."

"This is not a military matter," Dane said sharply, "or else they would have sent my orderly. Come, come, Sergeant, what is it? Don't stand there dumb, man. Speak up and be off."

Joe Moses let a few seconds of silence run through the room, then he gave George Dane both barrels. "Sir, your wife is waiting at the hotel. She wants to see you on an important matter and if you don't go to her, she'll come here."

Dane swayed like a tall tree disturbed by the wind, not uprooted, but bent, and he put out his hand and found the solid support of the piano. Blood drained from his face and anger came to his eyes.

"Damn you, Moses, what kind of a lie is this?" He stepped across the room and stood in front of the sergeant, his manner threatening. "I happen to know —"

"Your wife was in Lordsburg, sir. I brought her through to Lowell, sir." He half turned and motioned toward the door. "My buggy is outside, sir. May I offer you —"

"You may not," Dane said. "You're dismissed, Sergeant."

"Are you coming or not, sir?"

"Don't question me, Sergeant. I'm waiting for your salute."

"I'll salute the uniform, sir," Moses said and came to attention. "You may expect me back in fifteen minutes, Captain."

Dane held up his hand; he turned to Señor Miguel Alvarez and bowed. "My deepest regrets at this unfortunate incident. Perhaps I should go along and settle this unpleasant matter. I won't be long." He kissed Doña Luisa's hand, bowed to her mother, then did a precise about-face and stalked out.

The servant handed him his hat and gloves and Moses followed him outside. On the wide terrace, Dane said, "I'll have my horse brought, Sergeant, thereby relieving you of the bother of coming back." He tugged on his gloves and clenched his fists. "And Sergeant, I want you to know that I'm not going to forget this."

"Don't blame me for your mistakes," Moses said.

"Say sir when you speak to an officer."

"Very well, sir. Go to hell, sir — in a hand basket."

George Dane stared at him carefully, then spoke in a soft, intense voice. "I have often wanted you in my command, Sergeant, and I'll tell you why. I've wanted to break you. No, not your damned stripes; you'd get them back easily enough from someone else. I've grown very sick of you, Moses. Sick of listening to people talk about you as though you were something special. I'm tired of discussing the Apache situation with my superior officers, offering my opinions and hearing them say, 'Well, we'll see what Sergeant Moses says about it when he gets back.' Now you've gone too far, Moses. You've given me a

86

complication I wanted to avoid. My wife had no money of her own. She couldn't afford an attorney to contest the divorce. She didn't have rail fare to come out here either. But she's here and for the last torn-down barrier, I must thank you, mustn't I? God damn you, Moses. I'll fry you for this. So help me, that's a promise."

Moses listened to him, then said, "Well, Captain, if you keep that promise as well as you kept the one to your wife, I'm not going to lose much sleep over it." He started to turn and Dane grabbed his arm and Moses knocked it away, showing the man his anger. "Listen, I don't need much of a reason for knocking you on your ass as it is, so don't push your luck."

The Mexican was coming with the horse and Moses walked toward the gate where the hostler had left his buggy. Al Roan was sitting there, smoking a cigarette. As Moses got in, he said, "You and the captain looked like you were goin' to have at it. You want to watch him. If he wasn't in uniform he'd be a card sharp."

"He's got troubles of his own," Moses said. "What do I want to worry about him for? Let's go have a beer."

The detail from Fort Thomas arrived

before nine o'clock, a company of cavalry with Major Hargus commanding, and he went to headquarters as soon as he dismissed his men.

Within the hour, two more companies arrived. Captain Leverson commanded the Camp Apache detail, and he went into headquarters, followed by Captain Rainey from Camp Grant. The orderly closed the door after seeing that the whiskey decanter was full and a new box of cigars rested on the major's desk.

Major Fickland filled their glasses and lighted their cigars, then sat down behind his desk. He looked from man to man and waited. Major Hargus, graying and round-shouldered, slumped in his chair, weary from the journey and weary from the troubles that made the journey necessary. He glanced at Captain Leverson, a man with a clipped, dark beard and deep-set brooding eyes.

Captain Rainey, the youngest, still in his late thirties, shifted in his chair and said, "I'm sick of this. If we're going to fight, let's fight and be done with it."

"Can you afford to lose the men?" Fickland asked. He arched an eyebrow. "By conservative estimate, Cochise has over a hundred and fifty men."

Leverson laughed. "I can't muster that many men at Camp Apache." He looked at Major Hargus. "How many companies can you put into the field?"

"Five," Hargus said. "With supporting troops, quartermaster, light artillery, and —" He shrugged. "And Cochise would never engage us. He'd snipe and raid and cut us to pieces." He looked at Major Fickland. "My sister is married to a senator and she wrote me that there are questions being asked, like why a thousand armed men can't subdue a few renegade Indians?" He wiped his mouth with his hand. "I would like to suggest that they come out here and look the situation over. Of course it's a suggestion I won't make. None of us will."

Captain Rainey said, "Since I am still receiving dispatches and mail from the east, I assume that our Sergeant Moses still manages to get through."

"Regularly," Fickland said. "It enables me to include in my reports the truthful but ambiguous statement that there is travel on the road." He reached for the bottle and topped his glass. "Lieutenant Travis at Camp Bowie is in a particularly delicate situation. With his command strength, he lives by the grace of Cochise, who could storm the place and take it if he wanted to."

"I don't understand this stand-off," Leverson said. "I'll be damned if I do. He makes war and yet he doesn't seem to want war."

"It is because of this," Fickland said, "that I asked you to meet with me here. I have a few theories that I want to put to the test." He looked from one to the other. "Do you gentlemen have any objection to my inviting a sergeant here to express an opinion?"

"If it's Joe Moses, I'd welcome it," Leverson said. "I've never met the man, you know."

Fickland got up and opened the door to the orderly room. "Corporal, ask Sergeant Moses to report to me."

"He went to town right after mess, sir."

"Send someone for him and don't waste time," Fickland said and closed the door. "We have the better part of an hour to wait. I suggest you gentlemen freshen up and get a little rest. I'll send an orderly for you when Sergeant Moses arrives."

"You're a good host," Rainey said, smiling. "I like your whiskey and cigars."

Fickland had an orderly show them to their quarters, then he walked over to the infirmary and met Nora Frazer on her way out. He stopped and said, "Been visiting, Miss Frazer?"

She peered at him in the poor light a moment before recognizing him. "Oh — Major. How fortunate that I ran into you. Is there somewhere we can talk?"

"Why don't I walk you to your quarters?" Fickland suggested.

"Thank you, that'll do nicely." She fell in step beside him. "Malcolm is bearing up under the pain. He's very brave, isn't he?"

Fickland cleared his throat and puffed his cigar and hoped she wouldn't press him for an answer. He glanced at her, amused because she was so young and a little stupid about a lot of things. She held his arm lightly, walking slowly.

"I suppose," she said, "you'll press charges against Sergeant Moses. He attacked Malcolm, you know."

"No, I didn't know," Fickland said. "I've known Moses four and a half years. He's too good a soldier to double his fist at an officer."

Nora Frazer stopped and looked steadily at him. "Major, I don't want to sound as though I'm contradicting you, but I saw Sergeant Moses kill a man just like that." She snapped her fingers. "He's completely ruthless."

"He's a tough man in a tough job," Fickland agreed. "Did Mr. Baker accuse Moses of —"

"Well, of course not," she said quickly.

"Malcolm is too fine a man to do such a thing. I just know that Moses is responsible."

"I'll talk to Mr. Baker about it," Fickland said. "You've known him some time, I take it?"

"We met when he was on leave," she said. "Over a year ago." She smiled and walked on. "I know you may think it a bit hurried, but we fell in love very quickly. With the mails so irregular and Malcolm's duties keeping him away so much, I —" She glanced at him and found him watching her. "I suppose you know too. I suppose everyone knows."

"That he didn't answer your letters? Yes. That he had no intention of marrying you? Yes. That Mr. Baker is a self-inflated ass? Yes, the whole post knows it. And if you're not careful the whole post will know that you're without pride, a woman who'd force herself on a man." He held up her hand to keep her from speaking. "Oh, I know, Baker's to blame. He sold you a fancy bill of goods, and you're the one who's hurt, but it's a man's world and the woman comes out short. I don't like it but I can't change it, Miss Frazer. When we take a detail through, you're going back to Lordsburg to catch the eastbound stage."

"I just can't!"

"You don't have a choice."

"But I told them I was coming out here to marry him!"

Fickland gnawed on his cigar. "It's a lie and you'll have to take it back."

"How can I?"

"Well," he said, "you can't live with it."

"And I can't go back either," she said. "Major, a girl has her pride."

"That's not pride," he said frankly. "That's damned foolishness." He thought a moment. "You're not in trouble, are you?"

"Just what do you mean?"

"Well, the kind of trouble young ladies now and then get into."

She gasped. "Why, you're insulting! What do you think I am?"

"I know that you're a young lady without a lot of good sense," Fickland said. "It occurred to me —"

"Well, just forget it! And good night!"

She lifted her skirt a bit and hurried on. He stopped and watched her go, then turned back to headquarters. He went into his office and sat down, somewhat disturbed; a commanding officer always disliked these personal conflicts that upset the rhythm of his command. He made a mental note to have a talk with Baker, to get him to make a clean break of this and send her back; she could invent any kind of a story she liked.

Sergeant Joe Moses had come on the post and parked his rig by headquarters. An orderly sent him on in, then went to fetch the other officers. Fickland gave Moses a cigar and a chair, then Hargus arrived, and a moment later, Leverson and Rainey.

Moses came to attention, and Major Hargus said, "We're too tired for that tonight, Sergeant," and introduced the other two officers. "Sit down, Sergeant. Enjoy your cigar."

Fickland said, "We've gathered to talk about the Cochise situation, Sergeant. I'd like to ask you some questions."

"If I know the answers, Major," Moses said honestly.

"First off," Fickland said, "do you think Cochise wants war?"

Moses looked at him, then said, "If you mean force against force, I'd say no. You'd only have to take a patrol out of Bowie to find that out."

Rainey pulled at his lip. "You get through regularly, Sergeant?"

"Yes. I've never seen Cochise. When I have trouble, it's with the young bucks

94

trying to prove themselves." He smiled. "You might say that I play a game with Cochise. We understand the rules."

"That's clear enough," Leverson said. "Sergeant, now and then a patrol from here or Bowie goes through and escorts the stage. To my knowledge these patrols have never been attacked. Can you suggest why?"

"I think it's because Cochise knows what we're doing. That is, we're moving through his land with only the necessary men and goods. No one leaves the road, sir. I think you'd have a fight if you did because the Apaches are watching every foot of the way."

Major Harry Fickland smiled and took the stub of cigar from his mouth. "Are you getting the idea, gentlemen? Cochise does not want war. Yet he wants to deny us the use of his land. He wants to keep the white man out, the towns out, the cattle out. And I'd say he's doing a damned good job of it." He ground out his cigar in a glass dish. "Joe, let me ask you one more question: Could we win a war with Cochise?" He swept his hand to include those present. "The combined commands in an all-out sweep."

For a moment Joe Moses sat there and

thought of the mountains where Cochise lived and roamed. "I don't think we could do it, sir," he said. "He knows every pass, every water hole, and we don't. I don't want to sound disloyal, but the cavalry only moves fast when compared to infantry or artillery. The Apaches would run rings around us and cut us to pieces." He shook his head. "Can I offer an opinion, Major?"

"Yes."

"I think we'd better make peace with Cochise."

"How in hell are you going to arrange that?" Rainey asked.

Moses shrugged. "Sir, I don't know, but it's going to have to be done. And when you make a treaty, make one you can stick to. Our reputation with the Apaches, goin' all the way back to Chief Mangas Coloradas, isn't too good. All along we've lied and taken what we wanted and blamed them for all the trouble." He scratched the back of his head. "Fact is, if a certain lieutenant hadn't hung some Apaches, Cochise wouldn't be raising hell."

"I don't think we need go into that," Major Hargus said quickly. "However, Sergeant, your point is well taken. Personally, I would favor a strong offensive against the Apaches. I don't believe they can be

96

trusted and I believe that any peace made will be of short duration. However, war right now seems a bit too expensive."

Fickland looked at Rainey and Leverson. "Gentlemen, do you have something to say?"

Rainey shrugged. "I'm inclined to go along with peace negotiations. But who's going to approach Cochise? Who's going to risk being roasted alive to make the first move?"

"Before we go further with this, gentlemen," Fickland said, "let's make sure we understand each other." He turned his chair around so that he partially faced the wall map; he picked up a pointer and tapped it against the spot where Camp Bowie stood. "All this land, sweeping westward from the pass, and north, is the domain of Cochise. There's water there, timber, rich valleys. In short, it's a very valuable piece of Arizona real estate. We must be honest with each other even if we can't be with the Apaches. We want more than a road through there. We want his land."

Rainey said, a bit uneasily, "Major, that's not for us to decide, is it?"

"Oh, be reasonable, Captain. It's always been that way. We don't want to live with the Indians. We want to run them off and develop their land. Look at Texas, and what's happening in the Dakotas. California's taken care of their Indian problem and Kansas is working on theirs. We're sent here to keep the peace, but it isn't peace we're really after. There are many people in the east, powerful people, just waiting for that dispatch to go through announcing the end of the Apache Indian." He stopped and looked from man to man. "What we are going to do — which is what we must do — is to make a peace with Cochise, then move in so many miners and cattlemen and homesteaders that we'll drown him in the flood. That's a tragedy, I grant, but it is what we'll do. We have no other choice."

Major Felix Hargus sat quietly for a time, then said, "I never thought I'd hear it put so honestly, or so cruelly, but it's the truth. God help us, it's the whole dirty truth."

Phil Rainey sighed and crossed his legs. "The man we send in is going to have to be pretty idealistic about this, Major. You couldn't tell a man what we've talked about and expect him to carry it off."

"He'll either be an idealist," Fickland said, "or a tough professional who can

98

bluff his way to hell and back."

"Or someone we could throw away, if this backfired," Leverson said.

They all turned their heads and looked at him, then Rainey said, "Do you have someone in mind, Mike?"

"No, it was just something I said." He laughed and brushed his mustache. "Well, we were talking about some damned awful things so I didn't think that was so bad."

"It's not bad at all," Fickland said. "What the hell, it's a fifty-fifty chance, isn't it? I mean, the bastard gets to be a hero whether he lives or dies." He looked at Hargus. "Make a suggestion."

"I don't want to," Hargus said. "You, Mike?"

"Not me."

"On this I keep my mouth shut," Rainey stated.

Fickland nodded and lit a fresh cigar. Through the haze of smoke his glance touched Joe Moses and clung there. "He's got to be an officer, Joe. Who?" He waved his hand. "All of this is in the strictest confidence, you understand."

"I don't think we should invite an enlisted man to give an opinion," Rainey said.

Fickland waved him silent. "I value Sergeant Moses' opinions. Now don't tell me you don't listen to your sergeants. When that day comes, the army's on the die-up."

Hargus chuckled. "That's a point I can't dispute. Go on, Sergeant."

"Mr. Baker," Moses said without hesitation.

"Who's Baker?" Rainey asked.

Fickland said, "A young officer who might not last long enough to get his laundry back if he isn't careful."

"I trust," Leverson mentioned, "that there was nothing personal in the selection, Sergeant."

"You wanted a man you could throw away," Moses said. "That's Mr. Baker. And what the hell, sir, he *may* come out a hero. And if he don't come out you can write a glowing dispatch and they'll put up a statue of him in his home-town park."

"Now that's very cynical, Sergeant," Felix Hargus said.

"Is it, sir?" Moses smiled. "I got my education in the army, sir. From the officers."

"I think Mr. Baker is our man," Fickland said. "Can we get a guide for him?"

Captain Leverson said, "I can recommend an Apache from the reservation."

"Pick him then," Fickland said. "Mr. Baker will be ready to go in a week."

Mildred Dane walked back and forth in the hotel room, now and then pausing by the window to look at the busy, noisy street. She saw Joe Moses come through the traffic with his buggy, tie up and walk across to the saloon with a tall, leggy man. Then she saw George Dane dismounting across from the hotel. He stood there a moment, looking up and down the street, waiting for the traffic to thin, then entered the hotel.

She stood in the center of the room, waiting, frightened now, and knowing that it was useless to be frightened. His step was firm in the hallway, then it paused outside her door and she waited for his knock, wetting her lips, swallowing so she could speak.

Dane didn't knock. He opened the door, flung it inward, then slapped it shut with the flat of his hand. For a moment he stood there, the lamplight making his complexion yellow, then he walked up to her and knocked her down with his fist. "How dare you?" he asked softly. "Just tell me how dare you?"

There was a trickle of blood from her nose and from her lips which his fist had mashed against her teeth. She ran her tongue along the upper front of her mouth, then slowly got to her feet, using a table to help support her.

"I want my sons," she said. "George, I have a right to them."

"You have no rights with me," he said firmly. "We made a bargain, Mildred. You've not kept it."

"I — I can't," she said. "Forgive me, George, I just can't."

He looked at her a long moment, then he laughed without humor and took a cigar from his pocket case and bent over the lamp chimney for his light. "You made the decision, Mildred. Isn't that so?" He stepped to her and took her arm and turned her to face him. "Didn't you agree to let me have the boys for three years? Wasn't that what you said? You wanted to be by yourself, to see if you couldn't pull together the frazzled ends of your life." He let go of her arm. "Get another lover, Mildred."

"I never had one," she said. "That was something you wanted to believe, George. Something you thought because it made you happy to think it."

"I believe it because you've given me

grounds to believe it," he said. "So Sergeant Moses brought you from Lordsburg? That's unusual; he doesn't like to carry passengers. I trust his price was one you could pay."

"George, you're an evil man. Do you hate me that much?"

"I want to be rid of you, isn't that enough?" He walked around the room, his hands clasped behind him, the cigar clamped between his teeth. "Mildred, let me put it this way: When I married you, you were all I could afford. I wanted sons and you gave them to me. But a man either goes up in the world or he goes down. I intend to go up. Of course you didn't get my letter or you wouldn't be here. I tried to explain why I was asking for a divorce. You must have left before the papers were served, although I can't understand how that could have happened."

"Perhaps it's because it took me four months to get here," she said. "I didn't have enough money, George. Three times I had to stop and work to get enough money to go on." She studied him a moment. "Tell me, George, does this Spanish woman really know what she's getting? Have you told her you're marrying her because she'll do until something better comes along?" A hard anger came into her eyes and she suddenly lost her fear of him. "George, I could drag you through the courts and make you pay dearly for a divorce, but I'm not going to do that."

"Most sensible," he said. "You'd lose and you'd be hurt."

"I didn't say I wasn't going to fight," she countered. "I'm not going to let you have your way. You'd better understand that."

His eyebrows went up and he smiled. "What are you going to do, get a job? I can take you over to Madam Lulu's house —"

She slapped his face, hard, quickly, then stood there and dared him to slap her back. Dane raised his hand slowly and rubbed his cheek. "Don't try to see the boys. Don't come near me. Don't make trouble, Mildred. I'll make you sorry if you do."

"You don't know what trouble is, George. Get your divorce. I won't fight it. God, I'll welcome the chance to get rid of you. But all you'll get is your freedom. The boys deserve more than you." She tipped her head back and laughed. "Really, George, without that uniform you'd be little more than a small-town politician seeking favors from the ward boss."

"Go back where you came from," Dane

said. "That's the best advice I can offer." He picked up his hat, went to the door and flung it open, then turned and looked at her. "Don't teach me to hate you, Mildred. Let's part friends."

"What?" She looked for something to throw, and he laughed and closed the door behind him.

On the street he paused, then crossed over to the saloon and pushed his way through the crowd to the bar. He stood there a moment, as though waiting for someone, then walked toward the back rooms, went down a short hall to a door and knocked.

He stepped inside. An overhead lamp shed light across a polished desk and a man in a pink shirt looked up. "You've got a complicated life, George. Sit down." He waited a moment. "Kelly didn't make it."

"What do you mean?"

"Joe Moses put him down. Haven't you heard?"

"No," Dane said softly. "Damn it, I was counting on him."

"Next time, do your own robbing," O. B. Calvin said. "Al Roan was telling the bartender about it." He scratched his cheek. "George, I'm getting impatient. All that silver just waiting for someone to come along and stumble over it by accident, and the only thing keeping it a secret is the Apaches roosting in those mountains. And I haven't heard any rumors about the army moving in and pushing the Indians on reservation. If it ever leaked out, about the silver, there'd be a rush and we'd have nothing."

"Don't tell me about it." Dane thumped himself on the chest. "Hell, I worry too, you know."

"You do it in a way I don't like," Calvin told him.

"That army payroll was a good answer," Dane said. "Fifteen thousand for me and five for Kelly. What the hell went wrong? He was supposed to be good with a gun."

Calvin shrugged. "All we knew about Kelly was talk. But we knew how well Moses can take care of himself." He shook his head. "I'm tired of waiting, George. You get your fifteen thousand and I'll put up mine and we'll make our move. We'll hire thirty men, arm them to the teeth and move into the mountains. If the Apaches show up, we'll give the buzzards the best meal they've ever had." He leaned forward and placed his hands flat on the desk. "I play for keeps, George, and losing gripes my ass."

"After I marry —"

Calvin made a cutting motion. "Marry,

hell. Borrow from him. He's the richest Mexican around here."

"That wouldn't be proper."

"Since when have you been proper?"

"Don't criticize me, O.B. I don't like it at all."

"You're as touchy as a woman," Calvin said. He sighed and leaned back in his chair. "I wish to hell I'd get a letter from my wife. She's been gone too long to suit me. And I wouldn't want her to be stuck in Lordsburg; that's a tough town."

Dane laughed. "You? Sentimental?"

This angered Calvin; he came forward in his chair. "If you can't borrow the money from the Mexican, then steal it."

"Do you think I'm capable of that?" Dane asked stiffly.

"You'd do anything if it meant something for you," Calvin said frankly. "George, don't think for a minute that I really trust you. You need me, but you lie awake nights trying to figure out ways to cut me out. Don't do that, George, because I'd have to shoot you if you did. You understand? Don't be cute with me. I'm not a man who'd let you get away with it."

"If you did that, O.B., how would you find the silver?"

"Listen to me, George. I love money. I

love it so much that the greatest thing I can think of is to sit and count it and run my hands through it and spend it, but that's only with money I have. We're talking about money I don't have yet, so it's not quite the same. You see my point? Don't give me any reason to step on you. I'd step hard. You've got your damned career and you don't want to be openly involved. All right, I'll front for you, for my share. But you play it straight with me, George. You can lie to your women and the army and the world, but you play nice with me. You do that and you may be both rich and Territorial Governor. But I ought to warn you; that's going to be your downfall, trying to be two things at one time."

This stung Dane, and he said, "Calvin, the first time I saw you I knew you could be bought."

"Sure, 'cuz I showed you my price tag. But I seen yours too. Mine's money, and I don't pretend otherwise." He pointed his finger. "You get your hands on thirty thousand dollars, George. When I move, I want to move big and move to stay. I want my own private army to fight the Apaches while I dig that silver out of the mountain. So *you* get the money, huh, George?"

"I need help."

O. B. Calvin shook his head. "Do it yourself. You're just wasting time. I'll give you thirty days."

"Now wait a minute —" He stopped. "All right, I'll do my best."

"You do that," Calvin said and watched Dane leave.

Mounting his horse, George Dane slowly rode back to the Alvarez rancho, mulling over in his mind the things Calvin had said. He didn't like Calvin, yet he was cutting the man in because there wasn't anything else he could do, save resign his commission and go it alone, and he knew he couldn't do that. Dane had personal ambitions, and a captain with a private fortune wouldn't stay a captain long, yet getting the fortune wasn't a matter of taking it. No one went into Cochise's stronghold and took anything, not without a war, not unless he was invited there.

Finding the silver had been a fluke; they'd camped the night on it and he'd recognized the rock formations and put a few samples in his saddlebag. While on leave, he had an eastern assayer test the samples, then he knew what he really had.

The riches were there, if he could only go back and get them. But not alone. A man wouldn't last a week in that country.

It was like O. B. Calvin said; you took an army with you and that cost money.

Which he didn't have.

Jim Ketchel ate the last of the beans and threw the can away. He looked across the fire at his brother and said, "If you've got any ideas, let's hear 'em. I'm at the end of my string, Pete."

They were on the south fork of the Gila and this was their fourth day in this camp; they had no place to go and had no intention of going south to Lordsburg. Pete Ketchel scratched his whiskers and said, "I've been thinkin', Jim."

"Tell me about it. I ain't heard nothin' funny for a week."

"There's no sense of us goin' back to our diggin's."

"None at all. She's petered out. Plumb petered out."

"Don't seem like much use prospectin' that country," Pete said. "Silver is where men ain't looked."

"Wisely said."

"If we go back to Lordsburg, we'll run into Moses again and I don't want no trouble with him."

"Be a shame to kill him," Jim admitted. "I don't want to do that."

"We've got our gear," Pete said. "Let's have a look in the mountains to the west."

Jim Ketchel raised his head quickly. "Apache country?"

"Why not? Ain't you smarter than an Injun?"

"Always thought I was."

"We're flat busted. Abe Wichles might stake us."

"I don't know about goin' back there," Jim said.

"Got a better idea?"

"Nope."

"I figure that Moses don't do anythin' out of the ordinary, and he camps in that country all the time," Pete said. "He watches himself, camps cold and moves a lot without leavin' sign. We can do it too, if we put a mind to it."

"I sure don't feel like goin' to work for anyone else," Jim said. "You want I should saddle up?"

"Might as well," Pete said. "We can reach Wichles' place by morning."

Abe Wichles was emptying his slop bucket when he saw the two Ketchel brothers in the distance, coming toward the station in the first pale light of day. He rinsed his bucket and took it back inside, leaned his rifle just inside the door and waited there, ready to grab it if this turned out to be trouble.

The Mexicans were feeding the stock; they were around back by the corral when the Ketchel boys dismounted.

"If we ain't too late," Jim said, "we could do a spot of work before breakfast."

"There's wood to fetch," Abe said. "Thought you boys would be a far piece from here by now."

"We wanted to talk to you," Pete said. "We'll fetch the wood first though."

Wichles built the fire and did the cooking. He was a poor man with food preparation, but when he cooked it was because he knew what went into the meals and if they tasted bad, he found he could still eat.

The Mexicans ate in their own part of the station; Wichles shared his table with the Ketchel boys. "Joe Moses is going to be put out to find out you're still around," Abe said. "He done you a favor, figurin' you had sense enough to appreciate it."

"It ain't that we don't," Pete said. "But we want to work another claim, if we can find anythin' to work."

"That's why we come to you," Jim said. "Would you stake us, Abe? Food's all we're askin'."

"Boys, I'd like to, but you're wastin' your time. Mexico's about played out, unless you want to go way south." Wichles shook his head. "I hate to put my money on a dead horse, boys. And to be honest, I'm surprised to see you took as much as you did out of your mine."

"We was thinkin' of goin' west," Jim said.

Wichles stopped gumming his food. "Aw now, fellas, you want to get killed?"

"We think we can stay alive," Pete said. "How about it, Abe? Will you stake us?"

"I should turn you down. I'd hate to have it on my conscience."

"How the hell are we goin' to find out if we don't go?" Pete asked. "Abe, you wouldn't turn down two broke, hungry fellas, would you?"

"Whatcha need?"

"Dried meat, hardtack, dried beans," Jim said. "No coffee. Couldn't make it anyway. Apaches would smell it a mile. And we couldn't dump the grounds." He reached out and took Wichles by the arm. "Come on, Abe. You can spare it."

"I'll give you enough for thirty days."

"Sixty."

"Aw, now —"

"Come on, sixty," Pete prompted.

Wichles thought about it, then nodded.

"All right, but I'll be sorry for it."

"If we find anything, you'll get a share," Jim Ketchel promised. "Ain't that right, Pete?"

"That's right."

Sergeant Joe Moses did not get back to town much before midnight. He put up his buggy in the carriage sheds behind the hotel and used the back entrance.

Although activity on the street had not slacked off, the second floor of the hotel was quiet as he walked along the hall to Mildred Dane's room and knocked lightly.

He heard the bed springs squeak, then her step and her soft voice. "Who is it?"

"Joe Moses."

She shot the bolt back and he opened the door. She went across the room to the bed and stretched out on it, her face turned away from him. The lamp was turned down and barely cast a yellow glow in the dark corners.

Moses turned the lamp up and said, "I didn't know when you wanted to go back or —"

She rolled over on her back, her arm up over her eyes, laying a deep shadow over her face. "I thought I might stay in town a few days, Joe. Too bad you had to

114

make another trip in."

"No trouble," he said. "You're sure you want to stay?"

"Yes, I'm sure."

Moses sat down on the edge of the bed. "You two reached an agreement then?"

"Yes, it worked out very nicely," she said.

He reached out and took her wrist and pulled her hand away from her face. "You're lying, Mildred. George wouldn't give a damned inch. Look at me when I'm talking to you."

She shook her head and he reached out, cupped her chin in his hand and turned her face so that the lamplight fell on it. Then he saw her swollen lip and the bruise puffing her nose. "Did he do that?"

She nodded and pulled her face away. "Please, I don't want you to see me, Joe. It isn't easy for a woman to be at anything but her best." She took his hand and held it. "George isn't very sympathetic, Joe. Of course, he feels it's his right to be that way. He wants his freedom and he wants the boys."

"You're not going to let him have them, are you?"

"I don't want him, Joe. Any feeling I had for him ended three years ago. He can get his divorce. But he can't have the boys."

"I'll take you back to the post," Moses said.

"No, no, there's no sense in going back, Joe."

"Do you want to fight or whine?"

"What do you think?"

"Then I'll take you back to the post," Moses said and pulled her to a sitting position. The lamplight fell on her face where there was no bruise, no swelling, and he thought her very pretty. She had good eyes and a good, firm body and he had a desire to put his arms around her — and he thought that was about the dumbest thing he'd thought of in a long time, putting his arms around a married woman.

"Mildred, as long as you're still legally his wife, you're entitled to his quarters on the post," he said, smiling. "You can draw against his pay at the sutler's store and I'll bet if you put your mind to it, you could raise all kinds of hell with George Dane's peace of mind."

She thought about this, then smiled and nodded. "Yes, why not?" She swung her feet to the floor and sat on the edge of the bed. "I'm sure you have the right idea. We'll go back to the post tonight."

"I've got my rig around back," he said. "We can go down the back stairs."

It was quite dark and the back stairs were narrow. Moses put his arm around her waist to make sure she didn't slip and tumble to the bottom.

He handed her into the rig and turned out of town, driving carefully down the alley to the first cross street, and in that way keeping out of the heavier traffic.

Once they cleared the edge of town, Mildred Dane said, "A few hours ago I knew I couldn't wait another moment to see my sons. Now I know I can wait. You did that for me, Joe. You gave me back something that George had taken away, my confidence." She took his arm as they rode along, her head on his shoulder. "My father was a railroad man and he was pleased that George liked me because George was from a good family and the marriage would take my father out of the Bull Durham class and put a cigar in his pocket, and that seemed very important to him."

"What did it do for you?" Moses asked.

"Fulfilled a foolish girl's dreams," she said. "But like dreams, they had very little to do with reality. George was on leave when we married; he stayed thirty days and left for his camp. When it came time to bear his child, he was far away and I had no one. But do you know I thought this was the way a soldier's wife had to be, brave and alone, seeing her husband every year or so. Do you see how stupid I was, Joe? I even let him talk the boys away from me. Yes, I agreed to let him have them for three years, only I found that I couldn't wait that long." She patted his arm and sat erect on the seat. "I'll tell you one thing, Joe, I've got to get a job, be self-supporting. I want to hire a lawyer and they cost money."

"Why don't you worry about it later?" Joe Moses asked as they pulled up at the main gate. The guard passed him through and he took her to her quarters and helped her down.

"Would you care to come in?"

He hesitated, then shook his head. "No, I'll put the rig up and —"

"Come back," she said. "I need someone to talk to, Joe."

"Tomorrow," he said. "If anyone saw me going in or out of your quarters at this hour —" He shrugged and let it go. "Could you explain it?"

"Are you always this careful?"

"I don't fool around with a woman's reputation," Moses said.

"And if she doesn't have one?"

He laughed. "That makes me all the more careful." He started to step back from her, but she reached up quickly and put her hands behind his head and pulled her lips up to his in a brief, warm, wet meeting. Then she laughed and opened her door.

"Now that'll be something to think about, won't it?" She tried to speak lightly, make a joke of it, but it didn't come off. They stood there, looking at each other for a moment, then they rushed against each other, their arms going tightly about each other. From that they knew they were no longer safe; nothing would be quite casual now, for the knowledge was there that her marriage and his rank were no consideration, no bar between them.

He kissed her again, this time longer, and as he kissed her he showed her the man, the need, and the danger in him. She was not frightened by these things and her lips promised him rewards never offered to her husband.

He pulled back from her yet held her close to him. "I'm a fool," Moses said. "This is the worst kind of trouble a man can get into." Then he smiled. "But I wouldn't back away. You know? That wouldn't hold me back."

"I'm not just a lonely woman seeking comfort," Mildred said.

He nodded. "I know. Good night, Mildred."

Moses put up the horses and the buggy and went to his quarters; he tried to be quiet, but when he sat down on his bed, Sergeant Mulligan lit the lamp. The other two bunks were still empty and Moses said, "Didn't you get paid?"

"Aye," Mulligan said. "But I'll not have me freedom until tomorrow evenin'. I'll go on me tear then." He sat up and reached for his sack tobacco and made a cigarette. "Don't you believe in sleep, Joe?" He struck a match and the flare made highlights and shadows on his face. "I'm goin' on a trip. Personal escort to Mr. Baker as far as Camp Bowie."

Moses opened his mouth to ask him what the hell he was doing that for when an Indian guide from the reservation was coming down, then he closed it before he let Mulligan know that he knew anything at all about it.

"I'd go over the hill," Moses said and stretched out. "Blow out the lamp, will you?"

Jim and Pete Ketchel left Abe Wichles'

station afoot and leading an unshod pack horse. They left well after sundown and moved west through the pass, leaving it after they reached the summit. Dawn found them dry-camped and dog-tired in Apache country.

They hid the horse during the day and took turns sleeping and watching. They saw Apaches at some distance and this puzzled them because they knew that you just didn't see these Indians unless they wanted to be seen.

They talked it over in whispers and reached the conclusion that these Indians were not trying to sneak around, any more than a man would use stealth in his own back yard. This was their private part of the Territory and they felt safe here, so they made noise and raised dust and thought, What the hell?

It also occurred to the Ketchel boys that the Apaches would not be looking for two intruders in their own back yard, so, if they were careful, they might just get away with it.

But they'd have to be careful.

This was not easy. It meant thinking out in advance literally every step they took. They could not shave because the Apaches might stumble onto the dried lather or bits of hair. They could not use soap because it might put a taste to the creek water that a wandering Apache might recognize. When they left a footprint — and they tried not to leave many — it had to look as though an Apache had made it.

They were careful.

And they began to work south, taking care. Living this way, on the edge of danger, keen-eared all the time, ready to jump, run, kill, made them a little wilder every day, a little more cunning until they were the dangerous ones and it was the Apache who ran the risk should he stumble on them accidentally.

They found country that looked good to them and made a permanent camp, hidden of course, and began to dig a shaft, carefully hiding the trailings. The deeper they probed into the flank of the mountain, the more positive they became that they had really struck it.

Jim had picked up the first sign in the bed of a creek and Pete, when shown some of the rocks Jim had picked up, had agreed that they were in a rich wash, but the real galena lay much higher.

So they had climbed to the impossible reaches of the mountain and had burrowed into it and they had not worked ten feet before they realized that they were both very rich men.

If they could live to spend it.

Lieutenant Malcolm Baker reported to Major Fickland promptly; he was given a chair to sit in, a cigar to smoke, and a smile to reassure him.

"How are you feeling now, Mr. Baker?" Fickland asked.

"Quite well, sir."

"Recovered from your accident?"

"Yes, sir."

"I have a very important assignment for you," Fickland said. "Wouldn't trust it to another man." He leaned back in his chair. "I've asked Sergeant Mulligan to ride with you to Camp Bowie. There you'll await the arrival of an Indian from the reservation who'll escort you to Cochise, or at least into a situation where Cochise will find you." He watched Baker's face, watched the color go, and watched the skin go slack. "The time has come, Baker, to offer Cochise some terms for peace. I'll give you instructions as to —"

"Sir, is this a duty for which I may or may not volunteer?"

"Volunteer?" Fickland wrinkled his forehead. "My boy, you've been selected. It's a

123

great honor. Why, if you have the bad luck to be — well, a man wants to go out a hero, you know." He touched his fingertips together and studied Baker over them. "Mr. Baker, perhaps you don't realize the importance of this signal honor. Why, you can marry the girl before you leave and if you don't happen to come back, she's comfortably cared for. Surely the war department would pension her." His shoulders rose and fell. "Then too, there's the matter of success. You could come back victorious, Baker. It would mean promotion for certain. I'd recommend it myself."

"Major, why was I selected for this assignment?"

"Why?" Fickland stared, drumming his mind for an answer. "Why, indeed?" He got up and paced around, furious with himself for not preparing for this contingency. Then he stopped and faced Baker. "Why, you ask. Very well, name me a man more qualified? Just one man?"

"I — I don't even know what the qualifications are, sir!"

"Youth! Vigor! Intelligence! Fearlessness, Baker!"

"Major, I think such a mission is suicide, and respectfully, sir, I decline to accept the assignment." He smiled. "You might say, sir, that the honor really belongs to a senior officer. A first lieutenant or a captain."

"Mr. Baker, I'm capable of selecting a man suitable to the task."

Baker got up and laid his cigar down in Fickland's ashtray. "It won't be me, Major. Thanks just the same."

"I'm giving you an order, Mr. Baker."

"And I'm telling you to go to the devil, sir, because my letter of resignation will be on your desk in twenty minutes." He clapped his kepi on his head. "And don't tell me you won't sign it, sir, because I have four years of service and all applications for —"

"All right, all right! I know the damned regulations!" He waved his hand. "Get out of here, Baker. You know this will follow you, don't you? When an officer shows yellow —"

"Some will call it good sense," Baker said quickly. "Goodbye, sir, and you'll forgive me for not shaking your hand, won't you?" He touched his fingers to his kepi and walked out. Fickland opened his mouth to yell at him, then thought better of it and sat down.

Fickland knew that he could have Baker ground into little pieces; the man was still in the army. But he knew how useless that would be, what a waste it would be. Not of Baker, but of his own time and effort.

He'd made his plans and a good deal hinged on making a peace move toward Cochise, but he had to move now; he couldn't afford to wait much longer. Perhaps, he thought, he might go down the roster and select another man.

Or ask for a volunteer.

Of course, that was it. Find a glory-hunter who wanted to take a large chance for the big stakes.

Fickland picked up his duty roster and glanced through it, and when he came to Captain George Dane's name, he stopped and pursed his lips. Now there was a man always eager to distinguish himself, get his name in a dispatch.

He knew he could sell this to Dane. But he'd have to make it sound good, sound as though others were after it; that would hone Dane's hunting instincts.

And he'd have to move quickly, before word of Baker's resignation got around the post or in town. He got up and flung open his door and in a few words had his orderly dispatch a man to town to fetch Dane back to the post.

Then Fickland laughed and rubbed his hands and sat down to enjoy his cigar.

Franklin Erskine was a resourceful man and not without influence; because he worked for the government, he disliked waiting. He did not mind making others wait; he only disliked inconvenience when it applied to himself.

His destination was the San Carlos reservation and Erskine felt that this was an important assignment because he would be the first permanent agent on a new reservation where there was opportunity for profit to the man quick enough to seize it.

And he meant to be that man.

He was still furious with Sergeant Moses for leaving him stranded in Lordsburg and he swore to himself that he would have Moses' stripes for this.

But that didn't get him to Camp Bowie and points west.

Erskine formed his plans carefully, then set them into motion; he studied some of the saloon habitués and carefully made his selection — six men with a properly tough frame of mind. He bought them drinks, enough to become friendly without making them think he was a man who threw away his money.

He talked to them, learned their names, listened to their troubles, gained their confidence. It was his intention to form a private military company, suitably mounted and armed, to make a trip to Tucson. The pay was good and the dangers certainly nothing that six brave men could not overcome.

Erskine felt that in the end it was the money and not his logic that persuaded these men to join him. Yet he knew the value of public attention and made sure the publisher of the Lordsburg weekly paper had the full story.

For a name he chose "The Territorial Volunteers," and he had a sort of uniform fitted for him at the general store and insisted that all six men wear suits of the same color. He outfitted them splendidly with good rifles, several bandoliers of ammunition and, to keep the public eye focused on them, he conducted mounted drill in Lordsburg's main street.

Harry Spears, the stage company agent, looked upon this as nonsense at first, then he began to think that Erskine might know what he was doing and made plans to send a stage full of passengers along.

The stage, loaded with four men and two women, driver and express guard, left Lordsburg on a Thursday morning, in the company of Franklin Erskine and the Territorial Volunteers. The day was cloudy, overcast, and there was the hint of rain in the mountains, but everyone was more grateful for the break in the heat than concerned with the threat of rain.

Everyone in Lordsburg watched them leave, and the four-piece volunteer fireman's band played loudly if not well. Children ran alongside until they reached the outskirts of town; they turned back there and only the barking dogs went a bit farther.

Abe Wichles was very surprised when they arrived at his station. He had the Mexicans scurrying about, trying to tend the stock and fix more food.

Erskine stood aside with Wichles; he stripped off his fringed gloves and thrust them into his belt while the stage passengers went inside and his armed guard filled their canteens at the well.

"We'll stay the night," Erskine said, "and leave first thing in the morning."

Wichles pouched his cheeks and spat tobacco. "Hate to advise a man, mister, but you'd be better off makin' the pass at night. Joe Moses always does."

"I do not feel compelled to emulate Sergeant Moses," Erskine said. "As a matter of fact, I suspect that the man has a good thing going for him and is trying his best to protect it. My intention, sir, is to take my command straight through, in broad daylight, and if the Indians are so foolish as to attack me, I'll crush them, teach them a lesson."

"Pretty hard to teach Apaches lessons they don't want to learn," Wichles commented.

"The fault then lies with the teacher and not the student." Wichles took off his hat and wiped sweat from his forehead. "I have some military experience, Mr. Wichles, and if I'm forced to engage the Indians, I'll do so in a military manner." He looked around at the station, at the desert he had just passed through, and at the rupture of rocky ridges and draws he had yet to cross. "I also think some investigation is in order as to why the military commanders haven't opened this road and kept it open."

He went inside the station where the heat was trapped thickly and the flies droned about and everyone sat at the table, swatting at them and waiting for the meal to be served.

The two women, a young girl not quite out of her teens and her aunt, sat at the far end of the table, flanked by two salesmen. The women tried to look calm and demure and it took effort, for they were dusty and tired already and the heat was like a furnace.

Erskine clapped his hands and they all looked at him. "People," he said, "I have an announcement. We'll stay the night and leave after breakfast. The Territorial Volunteers will have an hour of rifle practice after supper."

Wichles, who had come in, heard this and said, "You ought to save your ca'tridges, mister."

"I'll make the decisions, thank you," Erskine said politely.

The Mexicans brought the meal, side pork and beans and potatoes fried in bacon grease, and the two women took a look at it and drank coffee.

Wichles had water taken to a room, and a large wooden tub that hadn't been used for a time; the wooden staves were dried and water leaked from it onto the floor. He wondered how he would call the women away from the table, but he was saved the trouble; they came down the short hall just as he stepped out of the room.

131

The older woman said, "We saw you carrying water and drew a conclusion, Mr. Wichles. That was very thoughtful of you."

" 'Tain't nothin'," he said.

"We appreciate it. I'm Mrs. O. B. Calvin. Perhaps you know my husband?"

Wichles smiled. "Why, sure. Been in his place many times." He wiped his hand on the leg of his pants before offering it. "Pleased to make your acquaintance, ma'am."

She smiled and took his hand briefly. "This is my niece, June Stanley. She's going to spend some time with us in Tucson. Her home is in Baltimore."

"That's a far piece from here," Wichles admitted. "Well, I hope you find everythin' comfortable, ladies." Then his pleasant expression vanished and his manner turned grave. "However, I wish you'd stay over here and not go on with this Erskine fella. It's my opinion he's askin' for trouble. Goin' to find it too."

"I *would* feel safer with the army," Mrs. Calvin said. "However, I've been gone four months and I'm anxious to get back. I'm sure Mr. Erskine will be careful." She opened the door and stepped partially into the room. "Thank you for everything, Mr. Wichles."

He nodded and grinned. "I got some eggs. Maybe I could fry you some." He motioned toward the main room and the buzz of talk around the table. "Luis fries everythin' in two inches of grease and —"

"You're very kind, Mr. Wichles. We'd like some eggs."

"In about a half hour?" He smiled again and shambled down the hall, walking on the heels of his run-over boots.

Later, after he'd taken the eggs and biscuits to Mrs. Calvin's room, he went out by the corral and watched Franklin Erskine and his men at target practice. Erskine had them firing from the prone and Wichles thought this was a little foolish; a man had to learn to stand up and shoot; he walked over to Erskine to tell him this.

"Won't be much layin' down and shootin' if you run into Apaches."

"The principles of good marksmanship remain the same regardless of the firing position," Erskine said pleasantly. "A bit of common sense will tell you, Wichles, that a prone man offers a smaller target than a man standing." He turned away from Wichles, walked down a piece and with his foot adjusted a man's shooting position.

Wichles watched the men burn powder and had to admit that their shooting was accurate enough; but he was a man who had lived his life in disorder and this regimentation somehow offended him.

The ladies were resting and the four men passengers were sitting in front of the station, watching the last of the daylight go. When Wichles came toward them they stopped their quiet conversation and looked at him.

One of them, a big man wearing a miner's flat-heeled boots, said, "They make a lot of noise, don't they?"

"Man ain't the quietest animal I know," Wichles said, toed a keg around and sat down. "Noise gets kind of welcome amid all this quiet."

The big man said, "Let me ask you somethin', Wichles: is there silver in them mountains?"

"A man would think so. But it ain't the best country to go prospectin' in." He took out his cut plug and pocket knife and shaved off a piece and popped it in his mouth. "Ten or twelve years ago, when there wasn't all this trouble, I roamed those mountains considerable. Seen a lot that looked good to me. But not enough to get killed for. You just don't go grubbin' around in a man's back yard without askin' for trouble." He shook his head sadly. "I guess I won't see the Ketchel boys again."

One of the salesmen raised his head. "Pete and Jim? I know them. What do you mean, Wichles?"

"Why, I grubstaked 'em," Wichles said. "They were bound and determined to go in there and look around." He shook his head again. "I reckon they're dead by now."

"And maybe they're not," the salesman said. "I know Pete and Jim. They're careful men in spite of their helling ways. Didn't they take six or seven thousand in silver out of Mexico? And right under the nose of the Mexican army too." He leaned forward toward Wichles. "If a man could go in there, what's his chances of makin' a strike?"

"Good," Wichles said. "I'm not a miner, you understand, but I've seen some creek beds not two days from here that bear lookin' into." He made a sweeping gesture with his hand to include the mountains. "Be no surprise to me if a man was to find one of them hills to be near solid silver. The sign I seen looked that good. Hell, you can pick up lead in a lot of the creeks. And where there's lead there —"

The big man in the miner's boots said, "I've always been a man who's worked alone, but I'm inclined to take on some partners and have a go at this." He looked from man to man. "There's four of us. Two to work and two to watch. You mean to tell me we couldn't do it?"

"You're crazy," the salesman said. "Four of us against the Apaches?" He laughed, shaking his head. "Fella, if I didn't know better I'd say you were drunk."

The other two men, who had remained silent, looked at each other. One of them, a salesman for a dry goods firm in St. Louis, said, "You keep talking, big fella. I've worked all my life for a commission and an expense account. Right now I'm risking a lot to get to Tucson for maybe a five-hundred-dollar order. You keep talking."

Abe Wichles got up and spat tobacco. "You fellas be smart and go on to Tucson." He looked at them, waited for them to agree, but they sat there, saying nothing.

Luis knocked before coming into Wichles' room; he carried a lantern and shook Wichles to wake him. The old man sat up, pawed at his face, yawned, and said, "What the hell time is it anyway? What you want, Luis?"

"It ees late, Señor Weekles. You come. They are gone. Weeth horses and food."

136

Wichles pulled on his pants and boots. "Who's gone?"

"The four men, señor. I was wakened by a sound, but when I got to the stable, it was too late."

They went out and down the hall to the main room and there Wichles saw the note on the bar; he took the lantern from Luis and set it down and read the note. It was folded and some money fell out, bills totaling a hundred dollars.

This will pay for the horses and grub . . .

He wadded up the note and threw it away in anger. "Now that's the way to buy horses. Twenty-five dollars apiece." Then he scratched his whiskered face. "Damn it, I'll never see them or the horses again." He stood there, angry at what had been done, yet feeling that he was wasting it on men already dead.

The stage driver and shotgun guard came in, both armed. "I heard noise and saw the lamp," the driver said, looking around. "Trouble, Abe?"

"The four passengers you had made off with horses." He spoke to Luis. "Check the stores to see what's missin'."

The driver said, "They go back to Lordsburg?"

Wichles shook his head. "Silver

137

huntin' in the mountains."

"Well, they'll likely find it, and more." He turned to the door to leave. "They paid their fare straight through so the company ain't out anything."

"Except four horses," Wichles said. "Twenty-five dollars apiece; how do you like that?"

"You made your profit," the driver said dryly. "Probably bought 'em off Indians for cartridges and a blanket and put it down on the company books for fifty dollars."

"You think I'd cheat the company?"

"Show me one of you fellas who don't," the driver said and went out, the guard following him.

The talk woke Franklin Erskine and he came out. Wichles told him what happened and Erskine thought about it before saying anything. "It cannot change my plans. The Territorial Volunteers bear the responsibility of guarding the stage, not the other way around. We'll leave after breakfast as planned."

"Those fellas are goin' to get killed."

"That's entirely likely," Erskine said, "but they went knowing the risks."

"A man can know and still not understand," Wichles said.

"What do you want me to do? Go after them and bring them back?" He shook his head. "They just may keep the Apaches occupied until we get through."

"That's a hell of a way to look at it."

"Wichles, I didn't send them out. Now good night."

After breakfast, the women boarded the stage, Erskine's Territorial Volunteers took their position fore and aft of the coach, and they left Abe Wichles' station. He felt a bit sad, as though he were saying good-bye forever and he stood in his yard for the better part of an hour, watching until they were only a speck beneath a raised banner of dust.

Erskine expected to breach the pass by noon; his men rode with rifle butts on thigh and looked carefully over the rough terrain, inspecting the hundred places where Apaches could be hidden.

Studying the land, the mountains, the jumble of up-thrust rocks, the tawny, sun-faded complexion of this waste, Erskine was hard put to understand why the Indians or anyone else would want to fight over it. He supposed it was true that there were mineral riches in the vastness of this forlorn land; minerals always seemed to be hidden in difficult places, as though in the scheme of things the more incredible odds overcome, the greater the reward.

Yet it was a land of waste and nothing to Erskine, a vast heat-shed where the furnace sun constantly baked an acrid loaf and the only visible inhabitants were lizards and snakes.

They reached the summit during the severest heat of the day. Erskine should have paused there to rest the horses and give the women a respite from the dust and flies, but he listened to an inner warning voice and kept going for another three miles. Then he found a wide slash in the trail and stopped, putting out his guards and allowing the women to dismount but keeping them close to the coach.

There was a great stillness to the land, a soundlessness, complete silence and they were all struck by this and stood motionless, listening intently to nothing.

Then Mrs. Calvin said, "This is a very lonely place, Mr. Erskine. But I think you'll get us through."

"Thank you for the confidence," he said, brushing his mustache. "We shall certainly do our best." He swung his head through a complete circle, turning his bulky body to accommodate the movement, and studied the high ground around him.

He saw nothing at all.

"We'll rest here for a half hour then go on," he said and walked away from the coach.

Erskine did not find the silence of the land frightening, or even ominous; he thought of it as awesome, vast, deep, eternal, but it heralded no dangers to his mind, although he was positive that his movements were under constant hostile observation.

To assume anything else would be foolishness and he was not a fool.

Later that afternoon they stopped again where the land was less harsh and spotted by stunted brush and trees. As one of Erskine's men, acting as point, turned his horse to ride back, a rifle boom echoed. The man flung up both arms and gracefully fell from the saddle.

"Dismount!" Erskine yelled and dashed for the nearest cover beneath the stagecoach. He had no time to look at the others for there was a brass taste of fear in his mouth because he could see no sign of the Apache, yet a man lay dead in the road.

His men were deployed — he saw that — and cradled his rifle as sweat ran down his round cheeks. The women stirred inside the coach and Erskine spoke in a surprisingly calm voice. "Please keep down, ladies."

The driver and guard, having jumped off and taken cover under the coach, looked at Erskine. The driver said, "They're in the brush somewhere. I guess they'll rush us 'cuz I sure as hell ain't goin' out there after 'em."

"We'll wait," Erskine promised.

They did wait, almost an hour, and there was no sound save the buzz of flies. The heat remained strong and there was not a breath of air.

From inside the coach, Mrs. Calvin said, "Mr. Erskine, how long will we be like this?"

"Patience," he said softly. "They're as tired of waiting as we are." He continued his study of the land around him and wondered if they were as tired. The heat bothered him and waiting bothered him and he decided to make a test, so he crawled from under the coach and started to belly toward a nearby clump of brush. A rifle blasted and the bullet narrowly missed him, kicking sand over his face and shoulders.

He saw the haze of black powder smoke and fired into the brush; two others fired and one of them hit the Apache. He reared up, clutching the upper part of his body, took three staggering steps then sprawled face-down. Instantly there was a bedlam of shouting, animal shrieking and the Apaches rushed them, ten or twelve, brown and half-naked and ferocious.

Erskine hunkered down behind his rifle and fired as rapidly as he could work the lever. Around him guns thundered, bullets thudded into the coach and screamed off the iron wheel rim and the powder smoke was thick and choking. There was no clarity, no semblance of reason to the charge; the Indians ran blindly toward them, yelling. Some fell and some came on, and when it seemed that they would overrun them, the Indians broke off and took instant cover.

The sudden, full silence gave Erskine a chance to think and he looked around. One of his men lay dead. Another, farther on, was bleeding and kicking his feet, making a fuss with his dying. The stage driver lay on his side, eyes wide open, but he saw nothing. Erskine pushed him away and took his gun and ammunition. Carefully he loaded his rifle and waited some more.

He counted the dead Indians. Three.

Two lying in view of the coach and another by the brush where the first volley of shots had flushed him.

This disappointed Franklin Erskine, who had certainly thought that the ratio of dead Apaches to those of his own force would be higher. Only they ran so fast and dodged and bobbed and crouched; they were simply damned hard to hit.

One of the women began to weep and the sound was a shock to Erskine; it broke the silence completely and every man looked toward the coach. Then the Apaches broke from their cover, screaming in, shooting, running, and Erskine knew that he was not going to stop them, knew it in the fear-filled closets of his heart.

He was struck in the calf of the leg by a bullet, and then in the upper arm. Neither hurt but he found he could not use the arm because the bone was broken, the nerves badly torn.

The bullet that killed him he did not feel at all.

The Apaches ripped open the door of the coach and dragged the two women out and promptly tore their clothes off, hitting them when they resisted. June Stanley was too frightened to fight; she fell to her knees in the sand and cried and as an Apache grabbed her by the hair and jerked her erect, her bare breasts bobbed and this made them laugh.

Mrs. Calvin bit one of the Indians and was struck in the face, bloodying her nose and lower lip; two grabbed her and held her while a third ran an exploratory hand over her nakedness as though gauging the child-bearing life in her.

The Stanley girl was pulled to the ground and held with a knee to the throat while an Apache hastily shed what little covering he had. Even then the girl did not realize what the Apache meant to do until she saw the out-thrust man of him, the poison there in his loins.

When she tried to clamp her long, muscular legs together the Apache hit her in the stomach, driving the wind out of her with a painful *woosh*. While she had no strength, he had his way as she lay there, half-conscious, half-knowing, eyes rolling wildly as though her suffering were too great to express by crying out.

Mrs. Calvin was hauled down; she fought bitterly and was beaten badly about the face, but her fighting gained her nothing. She had no virginity to be torn away and suffered less — or perhaps she suffered more, for she lay with her eyes closed, hair strewn in the dirt, nostrils pinched against the hot stink of the man on her.

Afterward, long afterward, when the Apaches had had enough, the women were roped together and led away, moving rapidly toward some distant, secret camp. They stumbled along blindly, numbed beyond the reach of pain, and when the rocks cut their feet so that each step left its blood mark, they paid no attention to it.

The Stanley girl cried all the time, but there were no tears.

Just crying.

Captain George Dane reported promptly and was ushered into Major Fickland's office. He listened attentively while Fickland spoke, a glow of interest in his eyes, a growing excitement in his face.

As soon as Fickland finished, Dane said, "Sir, I accept the assignment, but I respectfully wish to decline the services of an Apache scout."

"Man, without a scout —"

"Oh, I realize that, sir, but I wish to take along the best man possible." He smiled around his cigar. "I would like to have Sergeant Moses assigned to me for the trip, sir."

Fickland frowned. "I hadn't thought of Moses."

"I did, sir, the moment you mentioned the assignment. Moses knows Apaches. God knows he's been outsmarting them all these years. There is no better man, and I'd like to have a soldier with me, not some Apache scout who is fuzzy about military authority." He looked intently at Fickland. "Sir, in past patrol action I've taken details farther into the mountains than any other officer. In accepting this assignment, I took it for granted that you would honor my request. It really hinged on it, sir."

"All right. I'll tell Moses."

Dane got to his feet and put on his hat. "I'll tell him myself, if you have no objection."

"Very well. When did you plan to start?"

"I think the morning would be soon enough."

Harry Fickland shrugged. "Yes, that's fine. Thank you, George." He offered his hand. "Ah — about your wife —"

"She'll be returning east with the first detail," Dane said, his manner brisk. "We had a talk in town. A complete understanding."

"I hope so. She's living on the post and drawing your rations."

This brought a frown to Dane's face. "Is she now? I'll have to talk to her again before I leave."

He left headquarters and on the porch he paused, a frown furrowing his forehead. Then he shook his head and walked toward the enlisted men's quarters, found Sergeant Moses' room and knocked on the door.

"Come in," Moses said. He was on his bunk and he put his newspaper down and looked to the door as it opened. Captain Dane did not step over the threshold.

"May I have your permission to enter your quarters, Sergeant?"

"Granted," Moses said and swung his feet to the floor. He pushed a chair around and motioned toward it; Dane closed the door, took off his hat and sat down.

"Sergeant, I've been given a special assignment and I've asked Major Fickland to assign you to me. He's granted my request."

"Oh?" Moses said. The lamplight gave the planes of his face a mahogany hue as he waited for Dane to go on.

"We're going into Cochise's country," Dane said. He seemed to be stifling a smile, fighting it, pushing it back, as though an unspoken joke pleased him greatly. "And I'm coming back, Sergeant.

148

You understand that? I'm coming back. Fickland doesn't know that. He's making the gesture and writing me off, but I'm coming back." Then he leaned forward and tapped Joe Moses on the knee. "You may not come back, Sergeant. Do you see how it is?"

"Before you sat down," Moses said. He picked up his sack tobacco and made a cigarette, smoothing it carefully before licking it. Then he leaned over the lamp chimney for his light and looked at Dane through the smoke. "What are you waiting for, sir? Me to refuse? You want to have me court-martialed? Is that it?"

"I'd rather you went along, Moses. You know that."

"I'll go with you," Moses said frankly. This surprised Dane and he showed it.

Then he laughed. "Of course, you intend to kill me."

"You're stupid, sir."

Dane's eyes widened. "What did you say?"

"I said you're stupid, sir. You're going to have your hands full and there won't be any time to worry about me. I'm not going to worry about you." He drew deeply on his cigarette and smiled. "Tell you what, sir; you're going to be too busy covering your tracks to think about doin' me in." He reached out and crushed out the smoke. "You've taken a few patrols in the mountains, Captain, but this time it'll be different. We'll go afoot. We'll leave the horses at Railey's ranch and go the rest of the way afoot. You beginning to understand, sir? This isn't a dress-blues parade."

"Moses, I'm the officer and you're the enlisted man. I'll give the orders. I want that clearly understood."

"Twenty-four hours out of Railey's you'll be dead then," Moses said and stretched out on his bunk. He studied Dane and waited.

Finally Dane said, "Fickland intends for me to fail. I don't intend that at all, Sergeant."

"Then you'd better listen to me. You want to be a hero?" He tapped himself on the chest. "Then you'd better let me make you one. Think about it, sir. All I'd have to do out there would be to keep my mouth shut and let you make a mistake. The Apaches would take care of the rest. It's my say out there, Captain. It's that or you just ain't going to make it at all."

"I'm not stupid, Sergeant."

"No, you're a real smart fella," Moses admitted. "Maybe too smart. You may smart yourself right into trouble."

"I'm going to leave in the morning." Dane got up and turned to the door. "Be ready."

"I'll be there," Moses promised and Dane stepped out.

Moses waited a moment, then sat up and pulled on his boots. Outside the night was cooled by a strong breeze as he walked toward the parade ground and along officers' row and heard the corporal of the guard at the gate passing Dane through. Moses wondered what was in town outside the Alvarez rancho that would keep a man there so much.

As he paused before Mildred Dane's door he told himself that he was a fool; he ought to turn around and go back to his quarters. He had just about made up his mind to do that when the door opened and Mildred Dane said, "Come in, Joe. I thought I heard your step."

He went in because he couldn't do anything else. She took his arm. "I have some coffee on."

"I don't even know why I'm here," he said, "except to say that I'm leavin' the post tomorrow. Your husband and I are going to see if we can talk to Cochise."

She looked at him oddly, as though he had just told her that all the quartermaster mules had sprouted wings and flown away. "George is going?"

"He'll be a big hero if he makes it," Moses said. "And he likes that idea."

"But why you, Joe? He must hate you. I know him. He can't forgive." She put her warm gentle hand against his chest and held it there; then she came against him, her lips seeking his. "Put your arms around me and hold me."

He obeyed her because he wanted to, because he could not resist her. Then he stepped away so he could think. "Mildred, I want you to go back home," he said.

"Why? I have a reason for staying now."

He shook his head. "Like it or not, I've got to bring him back. You understand that, don't you? If I didn't, what could I say to you?"

"You wouldn't have to say anything, Joe."

"No, it wouldn't be that easy. I'd have to spend the rest of my life asking myself if I had let him die so I could love his woman."

"I'm not his woman."

"In name you are."

"I hate that."

He sighed and blew out a long breath. "We can't have everything our way, Mildred." Then he smiled. "Did you say you had some coffee?"

O. B. Calvin was counting the receipts when George Dane knocked on his side door. Calvin picked up a revolver, cocked it, stepped to the door and said, "Who are you and what do you want?"

"George. Let me in."

Calvin slid the bolt, opened the door and quickly locked it again. He walked back to his desk, carefully let down the hammer and put the pistol aside. "What the hell is it now?"

"I'm a man with the damnedest luck," Dane said, flopping in a wooden chair. "Calvin, I'm going back up there in the morning, where the silver is." He watched the man look up, surprise plain on his florid face.

"A patrol?"

"No, alone. That is, Joe Moses is going with me."

"That's not good," Calvin said, shaking his head. "And I don't see what's to get het up about."

"Why, you damned fool, I can stake the

claim. Four little pieces of paper in my pocket for corner markers, that's all I need. Record that and we can sit back and take our time."

"I'm for moving now, with the men behind me," Calvin said. He studied Dane carefully. "What are you going into Cochise's country for? You can get killed here."

"Peace mission. Fickland wants to end the trouble, open the road."

"Well, I'm for that," Calvin admitted. "You didn't hear anything about a patrol going through to Lordsburg, did you? In the last mail, Moses brought a letter from my wife. She's coming back from the east with my niece."

"No, I didn't hear anything," Dane said. "O.B., I've got to get back. So let's draw up the papers and stake the claim."

"You think you can do this under Moses' nose?"

"Listen, I know something about Apache ways myself. Didn't I take patrols into those mountains and bring them back?"

"You were lucky," Calvin said frankly. "Stay lucky, George. And don't make trouble for Moses. You've got enough of your own."

"You wouldn't want me to stand in the way of a natural accident, would you?"

Calvin shook his head and reached for paper and pen. "You're so sneaky, George, I don't see how you can trust yourself with a razor to shave." He wrote for several minutes, then gave the papers to Dane to sign. After reading them carefully, Dane signed them and put them in his pocket.

Calvin said, "Are you going to leave the boys with the Mexican woman while you're gone?"

"She's Spanish," Dane corrected. "Yes, they're safe there. My wife can't get to them."

"That's a hell of a way to get even with somebody," Calvin said. He got up and unlocked the door and Dane took the hint and went out. Afterward Calvin shot the bolt and stood there, his brow wrinkled in thought.

Then he went back to his addition.

Doña Luisa Alvarez said good night to her father and mother a little after nine o'clock and walked toward her room in the west wing of the house. Her heels tapped daintily down the polished stone corridor and when she came to her door she stopped, reflected a moment, then walked on to the end of the hall.

She paused before a carved oak door, listened, and heard soft giggling. She knocked and bed springs squeaked and a voice said, "Come in, please."

She opened the door. The Dane boys were in bed, covers pulled to their chins. They looked at her with large brown eyes and the oldest said, "We were just falling asleep, Doña Luisa."

"Yes, I heard you laughing about it." She sat down on the edge of Richard's bed and clasped her hands firmly in her lap. "Do you miss your mother?"

Richard nodded solemnly and glanced at Tad. "Now don't start snifflin'. He cries sometimes when he thinks about her."

"You know that I want you to be my boys, don't you?"

"Yes'm," Richard said. "I guess you're going to be. Father says so all the time."

"But you love your mother?"

"Yes'm. In spite of what he says, we remember her. And I guess it's not her fault that she didn't come out here to us. Don't you think that's so, Doña Luisa? Don't you think it's because something happened to her and not because she didn't want us?"

She studied the boy for a moment, then lowered her eyes. "I love your father and I want to be his wife. But I want you to be happy too."

"I guess we are," Richard said. He looked at his younger brother. "Aren't you happy, Tad?"

"Most of the time I am," Tad admitted. "But I miss her, Doña Luisa. Even when Father says I'll get over it, I know I won't. Is that wrong?"

"So much is wrong," Doña Luisa Alvarez said, "that I don't know what is really right." She got up and seemed excited. "Boys, get dressed quietly. I'll wait in the hall."

Richard's eyes got round. "Where are we going?"

"I'm going to take you to your mother," she said quickly. "That will make your father very angry, but it can't be helped. I'm not going to make two boys pay for my happiness. God would never forgive me, even if I learned to forgive myself."

"But she's —"

"She's here, Richard. At the army post. Now get dressed and be quiet and please hurry."

She stepped out into the hall but as she did not completely close the door, she heard them scampering into their clothes. Then Richard came out, tugging his cap in place, and Tad crowded against his back as though all this was a fearful bit of doing and he wasn't completely sure he should be a part of it.

Doña Luisa stopped at her room for a wrap, then they left the house by a side door and went to the stables. She had never harnessed a team in her life and Richard had to do it for her. He handed her into the buggy and drove, enjoying this manly role. When they got to the gate, the servant there seemed surprised.

"It is late," he said as a warning.

"I know the time, Jesus. Open the gate, please."

He did because it was an order. They passed through and he closed it and stood there, wondering if he should desert his post to let the *segundo* know of this or wait until he was relieved.

He decided to wait.

Richard knew the road and kept the team pacing briskly. He was just old enough to have picked up some mature ways, like keeping his mouth shut when questions were just bubbling in his mind.

Tad hadn't learned this; he said, "Doña Luisa, how do you know my mother's here?"

"Because a soldier came to the house and told your father. They left together. That's how I know." She reached out and patted his head. "I don't blame your father for wanting you for himself. You're dear boys, but there is wrong in this. It's something one feels in the heart. Now, no more talking. Can you drive faster, Richard?"

An orderly knocked on Mildred Dane's door; she fumbled for matches to light the lamp and looked at her watch; it was a little after eleven o'clock and the post was nearly silent.

"Who is it?"

"Guardhouse orderly, ma'am. There's a Spanish woman at the gate with two boys. She says they're yours."

Mildred Dane felt her blood pump wildly in the veins at her temples as she hurriedly slipped into her robe. "Will you send them here, please?"

She rushed to the dresser and the mirror, fussing with her hair, and wishing she looked prettier, wishing she had a little more time, just a few minutes to powder away the shine on her nose and put a damp cloth to her eyes to take away the puffiness of sleep. She was afraid she would cry and that would make them red and horrible. She heard the buggy stop outside, turned and put out a hand to the dresser top to support herself — her legs felt that weak.

Then the door opened and Tad stood there, taller than she remembered, little Theodore with his big eyes and cowlick and large front teeth.

"Tad," she said. "My darling Tad."

He began to cry without screwing up his face the way he always did; he cried as a man cries, with the tears just spilling down his cheeks. Then they rushed toward each other and she fell on her knees, hurting them on the hardwood floor and not minding; they had their arms around each other and she kissed him again and again.

Richard came in, came up to her and put his hand on her head. She looked at him; he was so tall, so straight, so big now.

He said, "The floor is cold, Mummy," and helped her to her feet, his arms around her. Then he kissed her cheek and made her sit down.

She laughed and dried her eyes on the sleeve of her robe. He smiled and said, "I want to thank Doña Luisa."

"No," she said, "I want to do that." She stepped to the door but saw no one. She went out to the edge of the walk and looked around at the dark, still parade ground; there was no one in sight. She slowly turned, went back inside and closed the door.

"Tomorrow," she said, "I'll go to her and thank her for what she's done." She looked at them, standing there, different than she remembered, yet the same — her blood, her pain. "My, you've grown." She wanted to ask if they had missed her, if they had thought of her, but she held this back.

Richard said, "We didn't know you were here, Mum. When Doña Luisa told us, we got dressed and came right away."

"Can we stay?" Tad asked. "I like Doña Luisa but I'd rather stay with you, Mum."

"Yes, yes, you can stay here," she said and went to them and put her arms around them, holding them close. "I don't know how, but I want you to stay with me forever."

Sergeant Moses woke just before dawn, shaved carefully, then went to the mess hall a good forty minutes before the call; the mess sergeant knew that Moses was leaving and served him breakfast. Afterward Moses went to the supply sergeant to draw four pairs of wool socks.

In his quarters he changed out of his uniform and put on a gray cotton shirt and a pair of tan canvas pants. He sat down and put on a pair of laced hunting boots. The socks he folded and put in various pockets, then he picked up a canvas shell belt and filled it with shotgun shells. That was his weapon, one sawed-off shotgun; he couldn't be burdened with sidearms. Then he picked up his canteen and stepped outside, walking rapidly toward headquarters.

There was one orderly on duty and Major Fickland, yawning and scratching; he motioned for Moses to come on into the office. "I expect Captain Dane at any moment," he said, sitting down. "Joe, I don't want to see you get killed out there. That won't do us any good." He wiped a hand across his face, pulling his mouth out of shape. "I wish you could be honest with Cochise. I wish you could tell him that he's fighting a losing battle, a lost cause, that we'll run over him in time."

"He wouldn't believe it," Moses said. Steps came through the outer office and George Dane walked in.

"Wouldn't believe what?" he said, looking at Fickland. "Major, since I'm going to be the one who negotiates with Cochise, I wish you'd discuss the details with me and leave Sergeant Moses to whatever tasks I might assign him."

"Oh, come on, George, get off your military high horse," Fickland said. "We're going to trade Cochise out of his country for some cheap beads and a promise, so it makes me a little sick to attach dignity where none is due." He leaned forward. "George, I'm ordering you to go in with a white flag. I want you to get that road open and that's *all* I want you to push for. Do you understand?"

"Yes, it's clear."

"Once that road is open and people start coming in by the hundreds, they'll start spreading out and grabbing; it's the way people are, George. They're grabbers, takers. They don't bargain or buy or pretend to be fair; they just grab what they want and hope they can hold onto it." He shook his finger. "But I want it clearly understood where Cochise is concerned that we are only asking that the road be opened. It's pure trickery, of course, but we must protect ourselves for a later time when we'll press for a full peace and the removal of the Apaches to the reservation. We must be ready then with no betrayal on our hands. We must be able to sit there and look him in the eye and tell him that we asked only that he open the road, that there was no way of knowing so many people would come and take his land. We are, I believe, committed to a complete course of lies with this brave man. God knows I didn't start this manner of dealing with the Indians, but I don't like it even so."

"If it's possible to find Cochise, to talk to him," Dane said, "I know I can convince him that he should let travelers use the road."

"Yes, I know you can," Fickland said frankly, pleasantly.

This surprised Dane and he stared a moment. "Now, that's a curious thing to say, sir."

"Why should it be?" Fickland asked. "You're a conniving man, George. Lies spring readily and convincingly to your lips. You haven't much of a conscience, and your loyalties run pretty much to yourself. I know you're the kind of a man who can talk to Cochise, George."

Dane's face took on color and held it and when he spoke, his tone was brittle. "Now I know what you think of me."

"Don't let it bother you, and I'm sure you won't. If you come back, I'll write a glowing dispatch on you and you'll likely go up the promotion list though I hardly think that's what you have in mind. Your proposed marriage to the daughter of a wealthy and politically prominent family suggests that you have other ideas in mind. Your name on everyone's lips won't hurt your plans."

"You don't believe I could have volunteered out of a sense of duty?"

Fickland laughed. "That idea would never have crossed my mind." He stood up and offered his hand. "No hard feelings, George. It takes all kinds to make a world."

"Your philosophy sickens me," Dane said. "Your idea of the good life is to grind it out in the damned army and hope you retire a colonel. Well, it's not mine." He shook Fickland's hand and turned to the door. "Come along, Sergeant. We've got a long ride to Railey's ranch."

"You'll wear out your horses making that in a day," Fickland said frankly.

"From there we're going afoot," Moses said.

"That may be wise," Fickland agreed. "I'll look for you back when I see you."

"Ten days or two weeks," Moses said and went out with Captain Dane.

They picked their horses at the stable in the first gray flush of dawn, saddled and mounted up. Dane wore his uniform pants, but he had on a leather shirt and an old felt hat; he carried a repeating Spencer rifle and some spare ammunition in tubes, cased and slung by a strap over his shoulder.

In the saddlebags they carried enough rations for two weeks, and each man had a canvas half-gallon canteen of water. They carried no grain for the horses since they were going to leave them with Moss Railey.

They quietly cleared the post and took the Camp Bowie road; it was sixty miles to Railey's ranch. The Raileys were the only nonmilitary inhabitants between Tucson and Bowie, and they held their valley land only by their strength of numbers and ferocity of nature. Moss Railey had his own private graveyard for dead Apaches, and as it grew it became a place of bad medicine for the Apaches, so much so that they hadn't tried to raid the Railey place for three years.

The sun was high and hot when Moses and Dane dismounted to lead the horses for several miles. There was no conversation between them; they had nothing to talk about, and the things they could talk about would have only deepened the basic conflict between them.

Dane had a map inside his shirt and he brought it out, studied it a moment, then said, "After we leave Railey's place we'll cut northeast toward the Gila. I know that country because I've taken patrols into it. It's rough country, but it's a good place to find Apaches."

"We just want to find Cochise," Moses said. "I don't want to fight my way to him."

George Dane turned his head and looked at Joe Moses. "You know, you've been making a legend out of yourself with that damned mail run, and I've always wondered just how much of it was bullshit and how much was fact."

"You may get a chance to find out," Moses said.

They raised the Railey place just before dark and three of Moss Railey's sons rode out to meet them, tall, well-armed men who were very careful until they were sure who their visitors were.

Railey's buildings were sprawled in a deep meadow, surrounded on two sides by thick trees and fronted by a clear creek that had to be crossed to reach the main yard.

Moss Railey was a huge man, thick through the shoulders and chest; he came out and stood on the porch while his brood gathered about him. Two other sons came from the barn, and the women, his wife and three daughters, came out of the house.

Railey recognized George Dane, but looked curiously at Joe Moses. "Get down.

Your horses are about played out."

"We rode straight through from Lowell," Dane said, getting down and stamping his feet to arouse some circulation. "This is Sergeant Moses, Mr. Railey."

"You the fella I hear about that gets through the road all the time?" He stepped off the porch and shook Moses' hand. "I always wanted to touch a man who was either luckier than hell or smarter than hell; either way, I wouldn't care." He grinned through his beard. "Come in. About to eat and there's plenty more." He turned to one of his younger sons. "Take the horses and see that they're grained and rubbed down. Come in, gents. Don't get many visitors, but this week's been pretty good."

Dane was going to let it pass, but the remark stirred Moses' curiosity. "What do you mean, Mr. Railey?"

"Day before yesterday two fellas dropped in on us. Prospectors. I never seen 'em before, but they've been in the mountains. Hit it rich too." He held the door open so they could step inside. "Of course I'm none surprised. I always said there was silver there if a man could get in and look around." He introduced his wife and daughter. One was heavy with child and Moses wondered how that had happened.

Railey went on talking. "There was a time when me and the boys figured to do a little prospecting ourselves but we don't know a damned thing about it and that's pretty much Apache country, so we just hung onto what we had. I can't say's I've been sorry." He looked at George Dane. "Seems to me you should know the country I'm talkin' about; you used to take your soldier boys in there three or four times a year. You go northeast of here, followin' the line of ridges and —"

"I believe I know the place," Dane said softly. "Did you catch the names of these men?"

"Think I did," Railey said. "Kettle. Jim and Pete Ke—"

"Ketchel," Moses put in. "I know 'em both."

"The hell you say!" Railey seemed pleased that it was a small world after all. "Nice fellas, both of 'em. Been livin' like hogs though. No fires, no nothin'. But they hit it, a big one."

"I don't suppose they've staked it out yet," Dane suggested.

Railey scratched his unbarbered head. "Well, they wrote it all down on a piece of paper. I'll take it to Bowie so it'll go out in the mail."

"Then they haven't actually staked it," Dane said. "The claim is not recorded with the office in Lordsburg or Tucson."

Railey looked at him a moment. "Cap'n, let's put it this way: No, it ain't. But it appears to me that when a man strikes it rich, it's usually some place no one else has been before, or else it's way to hell and gone away from everything. Now, it don't seem reasonable to me to expect that man to make it to town easy-like and register his claim. He puts out his marker stones and does the best he can, like comin' here with his paper. To me it's registered and anyone else would sure as hell get shot tryin' to jump it."

Dane had no comment to make; he went outside to wash and Railey had his women make two more places at the table.

Joe Moses went out and joined Dane at the creek; he squatted down, cupped his hands and poured water over his head, shook it, and dried on his handkerchief.

When he straightened up he said, "Are you interested in mining, Captain?"

"What makes you think that?"

"You sounded interested."

"I was thinking about what news of a silver strike would do," Dane said. "Even Cochise couldn't stop them. It would be war."

"That's what the army's figured on all the time, isn't it? Isn't that the way it's always been with Indians? War?"

"That's because they're warlike to begin with."

Moses made a disgusted sound. "Don't be an ass, man!" He turned and walked back to the house and sat down at the table.

From the variety and quantity of food, Joe Moses knew that Railey had a good thing going in the ranch; when the country opened up and provided a market for his cattle and farm produce, Railey would be on his way to being a wealthy man.

Moses enjoyed the meal and the talk; the old man was full of it, and Moses supposed that it was lonesome as hell, seeing the same faces every day and hearing the same voices saying about the same thing. He looked at the girls; they were pretty in a square-faced way and the prettiest was the pregnant one, who now and then looked at George Dane and, when he looked at her, quickly lowered her eyes.

This seemed odd to Moses and after the meal, when they went on the porch to smoke, he thought about it while Moss Railey prattled on.

He knew that Dane had been through

here before and it made him think a bit. Maybe one of the soldiers had talked her into something.

Moss Railey poked Moses on the arm. "You goin' deaf or somethin'? I asked you a question?"

"The night air must be making my mind wander," Moses said. "I sure didn't hear you."

"I asked you what the army was goin' to do about the Indians. We can't go on like this forever, can we?"

"No, it's got to change," Moses said. "And soon too."

"I've been here eleven years," Railey said. "Buried four boys and two girls. Buried about twenty Apaches too. But the score don't ease my heart any. A man puts his blood in a grave and it makes somethin' out of a piece of land." He waved his hands. "All my boys carry wounds from Indian trouble. It's got to end, Moses."

"The eastern papers pick up some of the goings-on from travelers," Moses said. "The way they write it up, you'd think we fought day and night."

"Don't they ever send anyone out here to find out the truth?"

"Sure. Last year I brought a correspondent through from Lordsburg. We didn't even see an Indian and when he got to Tucson he accused me of building up imaginary danger so I'd get a promotion quicker. He visited the army posts and when he saw the patrols come back without having fought anyone, he accused the officers of tricking him, taking him where there wasn't any trouble. Now, how do you tell a man like that the truth?"

"I suppose he wrote that all up, just like he had it in his mind?"

"Sure. What else could he do?" Moses got up and stretched. "I think I'll turn in. The captain may want to leave tonight."

"Not tonight," Dane said from the doorway; he had just come out. "Dawn will be better."

"Hate to disagree —" Railey started to say.

"Then don't," Dane advised. "Thank you for the meal. I'll bunk in the barn."

"Don't smoke and set it afire," Railey warned.

"I won't," Dane said and stepped off the porch. He looked at Moses. "You bunk in the toolshed or anywhere else it suits you."

"You want me to blow reveille, sir?"

"Don't get smart. You're still in the army." He turned and walked across the yard.

Railey said, "He ain't too easy to get along with, is he?"

Moses shrugged; he didn't think his troubles were any of Moss Railey's business. He said, "Good night and thanks for the supper."

"You're welcome to it. And try the tack shed. There's some hoss blankets you can use for a mattress."

Moses was not aware of how long he had slept, but he woke suddenly, not sure what had brought him awake; he stood up and moved to the door of the tack shed and listened. Then he heard it again, a woman's sob, and while he stood there he saw Railey's pregnant daughter run from the barn toward the house.

That was enough to start Moses into motion, that and the fact that there was a lantern burning in the barn. As he hurried across the yard, he heard a man swear and the clear sound of a fist hitting bone.

When he stepped inside he saw Railey and his two oldest boys. The boys held George Dane's arms and there was blood on Dane's face.

"What's going on?" Moses asked.

"Nothing that concerns you," Railey

said, not looking around. "Go back to bed, Sa'jint."

"Now, wait a minute, Mr. Railey. Did you hit him?"

"I did," Railey said, ignoring Moses. He spoke to Dane. "I waited and I knew if I waited long enough she'd point to the man."

"My God, you don't think I — ?"

"She come to you, didn't she?" Railey fisted a handful of Dane's leather shirt.

Moses started to move toward the man, but stopped when another of Railey's boys said, "Now you'd better not mix in this like Pa says. I've got a .44 in my hand and I'll use it if I have to."

Moses looked around and it was no lie; a Remington was pointed at the small of his back. He said, "Are you going to shoot me, mister?"

"I'd hate to," the young man said. "I guess I'd try to put out your light by hitting you first. But if I had to, I would. This is somethin' that's family business, Sergeant. You've got to understand that."

George Dane struggled briefly, then quit. "Railey, you're out of your mind. Why would I — It's unthinkable."

"Let's add it up," Railey said reasonably. "Three times you slept in the house while your men camped on the other side of the

175

creek. Twice you used the barn, like you did tonight. Made some point of it, as I recall. Now my little Mary, she could hear you plain enough through the open door. You beginnin' to see how it adds up?"

"Did she accuse me?"

"Not in words," Railey said. "But she came to you. She'd go to the man that fixed her up." He shrugged his huge shoulders. "We don't hold it in no disgrace, her carryin' and not bein' married. Out here, where could she find a husband anyway? All you got to do, Captain, is tell it out to us so the little one can take your name. That's only right, ain't it?"

"You — you want me to marry her?" Dane asked.

Railey nodded. "It's the thing to do. You had your fun. We got to pay for it. We'll write it in the Bible and the next time we get to Tucson we'll have the preacher make note of it so it'll be legal. Now, we're not askin' you to live here. You got your life. Let her have hers so when she finds a man she'll bring him no disgrace."

Moses said, "For Christ's sake, Dane, tell the man the truth! Hasn't it gone far enough?"

Railey looked around at Moses. "What truth?"

"He's got a wife and two kids now," Moses said.

"Ah," Railey said softly, like a sigh. "Asa, take the sa'jint out. Take him in the house."

The man behind Moses prodded him with the gun and said, "If you're thinkin' what I think you're thinkin', remember I'm big enough to carry you."

"I figured that," Moses said. He looked at George Dane. "For once, do something right. Be honest with this man."

"You sonofabitch, I'll kill you!" Dane said and tried to jerk free, but the two Railey boys held him there.

Asa said, "We're wastin' time, Sa'jint." He pushed him with the barrel of the gun and before they were halfway across the yard Moses could hear Moss Railey's fists against Dane's face and body.

Joe Moses said, "Don't do anything you'll have to answer to the law for, Asa."

"What law?" Asa asked. "You behave and you won't get hurt. All right?"

"I can't promise anything."

"Then you won't mind if I stand here and point this at you."

7

Joe Moses sat in the kitchen and smoked and drank coffee. Asa Railey sat with him, the .44 Remington on the table near his hand. The women were in another part of the house; it was quiet and they waited until the waiting began to get on Joe Moses' nerves.

He shifted in his chair and tried to stand up but Asa put his hand on the pistol and Moses relaxed again.

"Now you tell me what good it'll do to kill him," Moses asked.

"Pa wouldn't do that," Asa said.

The squeak of the pump handle made Moses turn his head. Then he looked at Asa and said, "I'm going to walk out there and see what's going on. If you want to shoot me, then you go ahead." He scraped back his chair and walked out as far as the porch. The two Railey boys were dousing George Dane's head under the pump as the old man walked wearily toward the house. When he drew near, Moses said, "What did beating him get you, anyway?"

"Not much," Moss Railey admitted.

He went on into the kitchen and poured a cup of coffee, then motioned for Asa to put his pistol away; he sat down and rubbed his hand across his face. "Could I have been wrong, Moses? I don't mean what I done, but did I have the right man? It could have been one of the soldiers with him. She could have gone to him to ask about him, couldn't she?"

"What does your daughter say?"

Railey shook his head. "She don't. Neither does he."

"We didn't stop here just to visit," Moses said. "We've got some place to go, something to do when we get there. He ain't hurt so bad he can't go on, is he?"

Railey rolled his shoulders and shrugged and drank his coffee; Moses got up and walked out to the yard. The two boys were helping George Dane to the barn. Moses overtook them and lifted the lantern to look at Dane's face. It was badly swollen and bruised; both eyes would be shut by morning. Moses swore softly before turning back to the house.

He stopped in the doorway, looking steadily at Moss Railey. "You did just fine, old man. Just dandy."

"I did what I thought was right."

"That doesn't make it right," Moses said. "I'm leaving tonight. Tell Dane to wait for me here."

He got his gear and shotgun and the old man came out with some food wrapped in a cloth; Moses put it in his sack, nodding his thanks.

"I guess I've made up my own rules too long," Railey said. "But I still think he's —"

"You think what you please," Moses said and walked out of the yard.

He pushed across the broad valley, walking easy and loose, sure that he would be in the mountains by daylight. The wind was soft and cool coming down the valley, and he let the feel of it on his cheek keep him on course.

Moses didn't mind going on alone; in fact it made him happy. He didn't like Dane, didn't trust the man, and although he would not tell Moss Railey, he felt sure that Dane had been the one who got the girl in trouble. It was the kind of a thing the man would do, for he was a man who could never let an opportunity pass, no matter what it was.

It wasn't difficult for Moses to figure it. Dane was a good-looking man, with his tall leanness and his damned smile and waxed mustache; he wore the uniform with a swagger, and he had an eye that could wink nicely at an impressionable girl.

Sure, Railey had been right and it really was too bad he couldn't have killed the sonofabitch, Moses thought as he walked along. Only you couldn't go around killing people just because you didn't like them or because they had been wrong.

The girl would have her baby and Dane had had his fun and the old man had gotten in enough licks to satisfy him; the girl would meet a good man someday and marry him and tell him that her husband had died — and that would be the end of it because he loved her and would believe anything she told him.

He let his mind swing to the Ketchel brothers; he was surprised that they were in the hills and more surprised that they were alive. That they'd made a strike seemed logical because they were both experienced prospectors and had hit it before, but not on a big scale. If they stayed alive long enough, they'd both be wearing silk shirts and living in the biggest house in Tucson.

At dawn he was in the high country and found a nest in the rocks, ate his cold rations and slept for five uninterrupted hours. The heat woke him and he bellied down and had a long, careful look at the country. He studied it as far as the eye could see, scanning every upthrust of rock and every defile in four directions; then he took a swig of water, got up and walked on, staying close to the larger outcroppings of rocks in case he needed cover in a hurry.

Movement through Indian country was dangerous, but not impossible as long as a man stuck pretty close to a few rules. Moses traveled through difficult, rocky terrain so that he left as little trace of his passage as possible; and he stayed high, walking sometimes several miles just to avoid traveling through a draw. Never did he expose himself against a background of sky; instead he tried to melt from rock to rock, blending into the land.

Yet there were open stretches to cross where tracks could be avoided; when he was faced with this, he would work his way as high as possible and hope that the winds there would erase the sign he made.

All that day a thunderhead had been building far out on the desert and he kept watching clouds pile on clouds, watching the rooster tail fan out far in the heavens. Then the frontal clouds started to darken the sky and in the early afternoon the sun was blotted out and a wind sprang up, strong and heavy with the threat of rain.

Moses knew what was coming . and hoped for it; in any other circumstances he would have dreaded it, for he knew how furious these desert cloudbursts could be. But the smashing deluge of rain, when it came, would turn every gully and depression into a roaring river, and every living thing, animal and Apache, would hunt shelter and stay there.

And while they were being comfortable, he'd make miles.

He watched the rain come across the desert, flogging up great sheets of dust as it ran toward the mountains; then it met him, the drops big and fat and stinging against his face.

It came down in torrents, cutting visibility, cascading off the rocks, roaring down the flanks of the mountains in ever growing streams to fill the gullies with reddish, roiling water.

Moses didn't mind being wet; he jogged along at a pace that was almost a loose dogtrot. He picked the easy trails, not caring what sign he left, for the rain was washing out his tracks as fast as he could make them.

He figured he could make four miles an hour and there was a good five hours until dark. He knew where he was going, if the rain would just last. The storm could stop as suddenly as it started; Moses had seen it happen, but he didn't think it would be that way. The clouds had built up slowly and steadily and it might go on raining the rest of the night.

He hoped it would because it would make the Ketchel boys that much easier to find. They'd be taking advantage of the rain, gathering brush and wood for a fire and a hot meal; they'd done without long enough now so that it would be a luxury, and they'd be thinking the same way as Moses, that any Indian with any sense would be in his hogan curled up with his woman.

Traveling on the rain-slick rocks was dangerous enough; one slip and a man could break a leg and, if that happened, he was in plenty of trouble.

Toward evening, Moses, weary and muscle-sore, sat on a high ridge and, unmindful of the rain pelting him, carefully studied the land below. He knew where he was because he'd read the reports Dane had turned in. Below, where a creek wound through a slash in the rocks to form a bend embracing a small meadow, was where Dane had camped, his farthest point into Cochise's country.

The Ketchels' camp couldn't be far, Moses reasoned, and let his eyes travel farther up the mountains. His eyes followed a natural defile from the meadow, reaching up through a difficult but not insurmountable cleft to a wild jumble of rocks. Water roared down the defile and Moses considered this, knowing that if there was silver higher up, it would be brought down to the creek. And if there was galena within fifty miles, the Ketchels would find it.

Having made up his mind, Moses moved along the ridge, poking his way in the glowing darkness; when he thought he saw a cell of light below and across a draw, he stopped. It passed from view and went out. He backtracked until he saw it again, then realized that the Ketchels were camped in a hidden pocket halfway up the mountain's flank, and their fire had been visible only from a restricted view.

Moses slowly, carefully worked his way down. He wanted to dislodge nothing that would become a landslide, and the darkness hampered him and made his progress painfully slow.

He figured it took him two hours to reach the fringe of the Ketchel boys' camp. To reach it, he had passed some mine tailings and their shaft, well hidden from all view except from the ridge — and a man didn't expect Apaches to be there.

They were living in a partial cave and had a fire going and were sitting around it; they didn't hear him at all until he spoke.

"Can you spare some of that coffee?"

They jumped and reached for their guns and Moses stepped into the fringe of light. "Now, don't do that," he said. "Who wants to shoot anybody?"

They recognized him and Pete said, "Well, I'll be a sonofabitch!" He looked at his brother and thought about the last time they had seen Joe Moses and they waited for a clue, a sign from Moses as to what his disposition was.

He put down his shotgun and sack and squatted by the fire where the heat soon made steam rise from the knees of his pants. Jim Ketchel handed him a full tin cup and Moses drank slowly while Pete put some bacon into a black iron skillet and placed it on the fire.

"First hot food we've had in a spell," Jim said. He looked carefully at Moses. "How the hell did you find us? I thought we was hid better than that."

"There's a spot on the ridge where a man can see your fire," Moses said. "I'd have missed it if I hadn't been looking for it." He raised the cup and smiled. "Good coffee, Pete. Strong enough to melt the buttons off your dress blues."

"You alone?" Jim asked.

"Yep."

"Jesus Christ," Pete said and shook his head. "You do beat all, Joe. I suppose you're looking for us, huh? About that thing at Abe Wichles'?"

"That's over and done with," Moses said.

"What then?" Jim asked. "You've got me curious."

"I'm on my way to see Cochise."

"The hell!" Pete said. Then he laughed. "And you just stopped in for coffee?"

"You could say that. Moss Railey tells me you've struck it rich."

"Well, fat anyway," Jim said. "We figure maybe a hundred thousand dollars apiece."

Moses smiled. "It looks like I'm sitting here talking to a couple of silver tycoons, doesn't it?"

"Hell of a lot of good it'll do us," Pete complained. "I mean, the Indians on one side and the marshal at Tucson looking for us on the other."

"I didn't say anything about you two in my report," Moses said evenly. "Not a damned word."

They studied him. "Joe, you wouldn't fool us, would you?"

"Why should I?" He shrugged and fished the bacon from the pan. "It was Kelly's play and you got sucked into it. Besides, you may have been wild but you've never been dishonest. No one's after you."

"By golly, Joe —" Pete looked at his brother. "Just don't know what to say."

"Then keep your mouth shut," Moses suggested. "You boys got these mountains all to yourself, huh?"

"Kind of," Jim said. "About five days ago we saw buzzards circlin' way to hell and gone off. We watched most of the afternoon then went over and had a look." He fell silent for a moment. "The Apaches had caught four fellas. Took their horses and guns and left the rest to the ants. We couldn't bury 'em on account of that would have given us away."

"Did you know any of them?" Moses asked.

Jim shook his head. "Who can tell after Apaches finish? But at dawn we backtracked them a bit. They came from the direction of Wichles' place."

"You're sure?"

"Pretty sure," Pete admitted. "It figures that they'd stop at Abe's to fill their can-

188

teens and get a hot meal, if you can call his cookin' a meal." He sighed. "Well, fellas have come into these hills before and never come out. I guess Abe figures the same thing has happened to us. For myself, I'd like to surprise him."

"If the Apaches haven't spotted you by now," Moses said, "you've got a chance. You do most of your work at night?"

"All of it," Pete said. "It's slow work because we have to scatter the tailings, but we've tunneled fifty feet into the mountain, enough to know that we have something."

"When we go to the spring for water, we do it before dawn, so game will hide any sign we might leave," Jim said. "It's a hell of a way to live." He looked at his brother, then at Moses. "Did you know that a stage tried to get through? The first sign we had of it was when a bunch of bucks stopped at the spring around sundown. They had the horses and some saddle stock and clothing and all the guns and two women prisoners. 'Course we didn't go down to see who they were or pay our respects or anything, but they were women, naked, roped together."

"You didn't do anything about it?"

"Nope," Jim said frankly. "Ain't ashamed of it either. I was scared and Pete was scared. About six Apaches and damn well armed." He shook his head. "We've been here a spell and they don't know it. We want to keep it that way."

"You just can't sit here on your rich ass and let the Apaches keep a couple of white women," Moses said.

"We've been doin' that," Jim admitted.

"Ain't you a little ashamed?"

"Ah, shit, do I have to be?"

"You ought to be."

"I guess we are a little, but what could we do?" Pete asked.

"You might help me find Cochise's camp," Moses suggested.

They looked at each other, then Jim Ketchel shook his head. "Have some more bacon and coffee. Take a little silver ore with you when you go, but don't ask us to do something foolish."

"You think this isn't foolish, squatting right in the middle of Apache country?" Moses helped himself to the coffee and finished the bacon. "Which way did the Apaches head when they left the creek?"

Pete flung out an arm. "North. Cochise has a camp up there somewhere. I'd say a day."

"What makes you think so?"

He shrugged. "I've seen Apaches stoppin' at the creek at dusk, comin' from the north. They don't look tuckered, like a man will when he's been travelin' for a day or two. It's just a guess."

"I'd trust it," Moses said. "Well, when can we start?"

"Who says we're goin'?" Pete asked. "Hell, Joe, you've got no right to put a man on the spot like that. It just ain't decent."

Moses waited a moment, then said, "You two were always a pain in the ass to me, always riding your damned horses into the buildings and kicking up a fuss every time you came to town. But underneath it all I thought there was some man. In all the ornery things you've done, I never heard of a thing you ought to be ashamed of. But I'll be damned if I can see how you can go to sleep knowing there's a couple of white women out there somewhere with an Apache ruttin' 'em for all he's worth."

"I wish you wouldn't talk like that," Jim said. "Huh, Pete?"

"It's bad enough thinkin' about it," Pete admitted. "What could we do if we found the camp?"

"Maybe we could figure it out when we got there," Moses said.

"Ah, it's crazy. We'd just get killed. Then what?"

"Well, you wouldn't have to think about

it any more," Moses told him.

Jim looked at his brother and made a disgusted sound. "You know, I don't suppose there's a damned thing we can do but go along. Either that or wonder the rest of our lives whether or not we're just a couple of greedy bastards." He threw a stick into the fire. "Ain't that about the way you see it, Pete?"

"I kind of get the feelin'," Pete said, "that I'm bein' held by the balls while my hind end's being kicked." He looked at Joe Moses and laughed. "When do you want to leave?"

Lieutenant Jefferson Travis left Camp Bowie before dawn with fourteen heavily armed troopers. He was to escort the stage from Lordsburg and four supply wagons, and he didn't look forward to the ride and he knew his detail didn't either.

They wore out a hot, miserable day in the saddle, and toward evening the scouts, ranging a mile ahead, fired three times. Travis took the detail forward at a trot.

The stage still sat by the road. The leather curtains had been taken and now adorned some Apaches' feet as moccasins. All the leather strapping was gone, including the harness, and the maroon velvet seats had been cut out, some fancy cloth for a squaw.

The dead men were a bloated stink; animals and ants had done a grisly chore. Travis and his detail had to bury what was left of them, a job that made them all sick at their stomachs.

They worked until well after dark; then Travis told the sergeant to mount the men and they went on toward Wichles' station, arriving after dawn the next day, bone-tired, on horses that needed a day in a stall and a full bag of grain.

Travis called the sergeant over. "As soon as the horses are cared for, see that the men eat and turn in. No pickets or guards."

"Yes, sir." He saluted and walked away while Wichles stood there, jaws mulching his tobacco, his eyes amused at all this military folderol.

"You come from Bowie in one jump?" Wichles asked.

"We stopped once, to bury what was left of the people on the stage," Travis said. He walked over to the watering trough, took off his shirt, neckerchief and hat and unbuttoned his underwear to the waist. Letting it drop around his hips, he bathed his upper body and dried himself the best he could with his neckerchief.

Wichles' expression was sad. "I didn't think that fella would make it. Tried to tell him too. But he was stubborn."

"I don't suppose you got their names."

"Get 'em all," Wichles said. "Write 'em down in a book just in case. Good thing I do too." He walked across the baked yard to his station and a moment later came out with a notebook. He thumbed through the pages, then said, "Here we are. Franklin Erskine was leadin' the party. He had some men with him. Got their names —"

"Wait a minute," Travis said, searching his memory. "Erskine? I've heard that name. Let me see — Yes, Moses mentioned him. Erskine was an Indian agent."

"That's right." Wichles read some more names. "The two ladies were —"

"What two ladies?" Travis asked. "We found no women."

"I reckon the Apaches got 'em. They're after women, guns, and horses." He consulted his book. "Mrs. O. B. Calvin and her niece, June Stanley. Address, Tucson."

Travis dressed, his face grave. "I've never heard of the niece, but I guess everyone knows O. B. Calvin. There's hardly a soldier that's hit Tucson who hasn't bought a drink of watered-down whiskey from

Calvin or lost his pay in one of those honest card games." He wiped a hand over his face and his beard stubble whispered. "I can't mount my detail for another fifteen hours. We damned near rode the horses out to get here." He took a cigar from his shirt pocket and lit it. "And the need to hurry is gone now. If the women are alive, the damage has been done. And if they're dead —" He shrugged. "Got a room in the station, Wichles?"

"Always got room," the old man said. He walked with Travis to the building and showed him his room, then stood out in the open door while Travis tugged off his boots and stretched out.

"It seems a shame," Wichles said, "that the Injuns have got to behave this way when this country's ours. It is, you know. We got more rights than they have. No two ways about it."

"Who the hell says we got rights?"

"Why, we do," Wichles said, surprised that Travis didn't know. "We make the laws, don't we? Bring civilization, don't we?"

"What civilization?" Travis asked. "If the sergeant's through eating, send him in here."

"Sure thing," Wichles said and went out.

Travis closed his eyes. It was too bad the Indians had no concept of the white man's thinking, or his nature. All the Indians had been exposed to was the white man's lies, his thievery, his penchant for trickery, then it struck Travis that perhaps the Indians had indeed been exposed to the white man's nature.

And it was too damned bad.

Too bad that they'd taken a couple of white women, for it would set off a war that nothing could stop now.

The sergeant came in and saluted. Travis looked at him and said, "Sergeant, take two men and go right back to Bowie with word of what happened here. I'll write a dispatch and have it ready for you in four hours. I'm sorry to ask you to make the ride back with so little rest but time now is —"

"I understand, sir," the sergeant said. "Will Wichles give us fresh horses?"

"He'll either give them to us or we'll take them," Travis said. "Get your sleep now."

The sergeant left and Travis closed his eyes again. He slept fitfully, woke several times, then got up and washed his face before leaving the room. The heat was still thick and would remain so for many hours. Travis went into the main room, got his dispatch case and wrote for twenty minutes.

Then he went to the stable where the sergeant was supervising the selection of horses. Wichles was there and he said nothing as Travis handed the dispatch to the sergeant.

"Ride straight through and watch yourself," Travis advised.

"We intend to do that, sir," the sergeant said.

"I've written instructions and my recommendations," Travis said, "but if the dispatch should be lost, report what has happened, as we know it, and tell the officer in charge that a dispatch should go to Tucson and from there to all posts in the Territory. We'll continue on to Lordsburg and come back as planned."

"All right, sir. We'll leave in fifteen minutes."

The sergeant went back to his duty and Wichles chewed his tobacco. "Gettin' ready for a little war, Lieutenant?"

"It's not my decision to make," Travis said, "but it's been my observation that in the past more stink has been raised when a white woman was taken or killed than when a Mexican —"

"Well, you can't count Mexicans as much," Wichles put in. "I've got four here

197

and I'd trade 'em any day for one good white man." He grinned and mauled his hat around on his head. "The last big Indian trouble, fellas like me had to fight it. This time the army can do it."

The sound of the rain woke Jefferson Travis; the room was gloomy, the last of the daylight almost gone. His eyes were heavy with sleep and he washed his face, then left the room and walked down the short hall. Wichles was standing behind the bar; he had a bottle and glass in front of him and was looking through the open door, watching the rain beat his yard to mud.

"The sergeant and them troopers are in for a wet ride," Wichles said, "but they won't have to worry about Apaches." He pushed the bottle and another glass toward Travis, who poured and tossed it off. "I don't know what it is about rainy weather that makes a man want to drink. Times like this I wish I had a saloon somewhere. I guess it's 'cause a man just naturally wants to come in out of the rain, then he ain't got anything to do, so he drinks." He looked at Travis. "I'd say that was a law of nature, wouldn't you?"

"I never comment on the passing scene,"

Travis said. "I wonder how long this will keep up?"

"Looks like a good one," Wichles admitted. "Maybe a day. It won't take the sun long to dry things off, though."

Jefferson Travis looked long at the man. "Wichles, why do you stay here?"

"Why? Hell, man, this is *mine*. The company staked me and I stuck out my time and got the deed to this place. I own it. All I do own too. By God, I'll keep it too." He waved his hand. "There ain't another station left between Tucson and Lordsburg. I'm the only one."

Travis poured another drink and took his glass and went to stand in the doorway to watch the rain. A strong wind blew it in slanting, gusty sheets and it pelted and puddled the yard and wiped out the view of the mountains and the vast reach of desert beyond.

It did not seem strange to him that men would fight for this land — this dry, mountainous land — and that they would fight as hard for it as for some lush stretch of meadow; for land, any land, was the symbol of man's wealth and status. He'd heard Texas men speak of their ten thousand acres as a "nice little place," and he'd heard the pride in their voice. The man could wear rags, but if he had land he was something.

Like Wichles with his station. It was his, and that was something.

And Travis thought that was what galled the white man — the Indians claiming the land he lived on; the white man just couldn't see that at all; he found it intolerable. If the Indians would only stop claiming the land, the trouble would vanish.

Only the land *did* belong to the Indians and the white man knew it and meant to take it, steal it, and afterward he needed a reason so his conscience wouldn't kick up a fuss.

The corporal came from the barn, running, his boots flinging mud. He stopped under the shelter of the porch and shook water off his hat.

"I've got the horses in the barn, sir. Saddled. We can leave any time you're ready, sir."

"Bring the men in here to eat," Travis said, taking out his pocket watch. "Not quite five. We'll leave at six. A slow easy march should bring us to Lordsburg around dawn."

The corporal splashed back to the barn and Travis turned inside. Wichles had heard so there was no need to say anything. "Wichles, don't the Apaches ever bother you?"

"They did, once or twice," Wichles admitted. "But it's been some years now, and I don't worry about it."

"This could be an uncomfortable place to be if the army starts a campaign."

"I've never been comfortable, so I wouldn't know," the old man said. He went in the kitchen to tell the Mexican cook to set a large table.

Moss Railey wore an old cavalry poncho to keep out the rain as he trudged from the barn to the house; he stopped on the porch to wipe his boots carefully because his Maude was inclined to be fussy about some things. Two of his boys were in the parlor, playing checkers. The women were in another part of the house.

"Andy with the captain?" the old man asked. He got out his pipe and tamped tobacco into it. One of the boys nodded without taking his attention from the game. "How's he comin' along?"

"He can see some now," Ronny said. "The raw meat helped take the swellin' down."

"Get him on his horse in the morning,

then, and get him out of here," the old man said, sagging in a chair. He sighed and leaned back and closed his eyes. "Moses is right; we'll have some trouble over this."

"Then we'll handle it when it comes," Asa said casually. He made three jumps in a row, cleaned the board, and Ronny swore and rolled a cigarette.

"We don't need trouble with the army," the old man maintained. "We've got enough as it is." He fell silent a moment. "Dane and Moses didn't drop in just to pay a call. We spoiled somethin' and I'll miss my guess if it ain't important." He looked at his boys. "Wouldn't surprise me if we didn't have to pay for it too."

"We've got family to think of first," Asa said. "No matter what, that's first."

"I guess we've lived alone too long," Moss Railey said. "We've stopped thinkin' of other people." He heard a step and turned his head and found his daughter Mary standing there, round with child.

"Can I come in, Pa?"

He nodded and motioned for her to sit down. "You want to tell me somethin', child?"

"I just got to now," she said softly. "Pa, he ain't the one."

The old man looked at her for a moment.

"Put a name to the man then."

"Ain't it enough that I told you he ain't the one?"

"It might have been, but not now. Not after what's happened. I have to know now."

She looked at her folded hands. "He was here with Captain Dane, Pa. I couldn't help it, honest, I couldn't."

"Nobody blames you for bein' a woman," Moss Railey said. "But I want his name."

"Malcolm Baker, Pa."

"By God!" Railey said. "I remember him. A pleasant young man. Never said much." He laughed and slapped his thigh. "Wouldn't you know? They're always the kind." He looked at his daughter. "Did he say he loved you?"

"Yes. He was going to come back to me. He will too."

"Don't hold your breath," Railey advised.

"I guess when they stopped the patrols —"

"He'll come back now. Asa, saddle a horse for me. I'm goin' to Bowie."

"Pa, he don't know I'm — going to have a baby."

"Then it's time he found out," Moss Railey said. "Do as I told you, Asa." He got up and walked out of the room to one of the back bedrooms and opened a door. George Dane was in bed, his face discolored and swollen. Railey jerked his thumb and Andy got up and went out, taking his rifle with him. Railey toed a chair around and sat down. "Dane, it turns out we had the wrong pig by the ear. My daughter tells me it was Baker who fixed her up."

Dane stared at him through eyes puffed nearly closed, then he laughed. "Now you're telling me you're sorry?"

"It's the decent thing to do," Railey said, surprised that the man would think anything else. "My boy'll get your horse for you any time you're ready to go your own way."

"I want my guns," Dane said. "You give me my guns back."

"Well, I couldn't do that. In your frame of mind you're liable to get reckless and try and shoot somebody." He got up. "The joke sure is on me, ain't it?"

"You really haven't had your laugh yet," Dane said grimly. "Old man, you have no idea what you've cost me, but I'm going to take every penny of it out of your hide. That's a promise."

"Too bad you feel that way," Railey said and left the room.

He went outside to stand while Dane's

horse was brought around and he was still standing there when Dane rode out. Asa came from the barn and said, "You goin' now, Pa?"

"Changed my mind," Moss Railey told him. "I can smell trouble on the wind and that's the time a man ought to stay home."

As soon as it was daylight, Joe Moses and the Ketchel brothers left their camp and moved north in search of the Apache camp. The rain was only a drizzle and by mid-morning shards of sunlight burst through the breaking cloud cover; by two o'clock, the sky was clearing, the sun was hot and steam began to rise from the desert in gauzy streamers.

They stayed high, picking trails as they went, and always watching the canyons where hidden springs might indicate an Apache water hole. Moses knew that, in his own back yard, an Apache was as much a creature of habit as the next man and used well-traveled trails. He watched for these and crossed several, but still was sure that he hadn't found the one he looked for.

Toward evening, when the sun was melting down behind the distant mountains, Pete Ketchel, who was leading, stopped, hunkering down at the edge of a deep ravine. They crowded around him and followed his pointing finger, then they grinned. Below, following the line of the canyon, was a clearly defined horse trail leading in a northerly direction.

"You can't ask for nothin' plainer than that," Pete said.

Jim Ketchel nodded. "I'd say we're within five miles of the camp right now."

"Or closer," Moses said. "Let's keep movin'."

"I could do with some sit-down," Pete mentioned.

"This ain't a sit-down kind of job," Moses said. "We'll rest a spell and go on after dark. The camp will be easier to spot with the cook fires going."

"Then what?" Jim asked.

"Let's figure that out when we get there," Pete said. "You know I can't stand to worry about things."

"I was just askin' a question."

"Damned stupid question," Pete said.

They stopped talking and stretched out to sleep, unmindful of the sand fleas and the flies droning and biting. When they woke, the darkness was almost complete; they sat up and listened, all hearing something. Then they made it out, a horse moving along the sandy bottom of the canyon.

A lone Apache astride a calico pony

made his way easily along the trail. They let him pass, then Moses nudged them and they started to work their way down, taking advantage of what was left of the poor light.

When they reached the floor of the canyon, the darkness was full, an inkiness. They could smell the dust raised by the Apache's horse and they followed it, moving as fast as they could without making any noise.

The canyon widened for a mile, then grew narrow — a slit, an aperture between sheer rock walls — then it turned sharply and started to climb. When Moses came to this he stopped, motioned for them to go back.

They retreated for nearly a thousand yards before they found a place to climb and they were sweating and panting when they reached the rim. They bellied down and got their breath, then Moses said, "One way in and one way out. I guessed it the minute we hit the corner and the upgrade."

"So?" Jim asked.

"Let's have a look," Moses said and led the way along the rim. They found the camp in a box canyon, well hidden. They counted ten or eleven cook fires and Moses figured there were thirty or forty

Apaches in the camp.

This bothered him because he knew it couldn't be Cochise's camp; he had several hundred people with him and the box canyon wouldn't have accommodated that many, or even half that many.

Pete nudged him and said, "You suppose there's a back way out of that canyon?"

"Probably," Moses said. "But no horse trail, that's for sure." He gave it some thought, then turned to Jim. "My guess is that the camp's so well hidden they don't use the back door. Let's find it."

Jim and Pete Ketchel looked at him a moment, then shrugged and got up and followed him. Moses made his way cautiously around the rim but they found nothing.

He backtracked, moving more slowly this time, and when he finally stopped they crowded around what looked like a runnel made by rain. The exit was amid a jumble of loose rocks, a natural slash easy to overlook in the daylight and nearly impossible to find at night.

"We'll sleep the night out here," Moses said. "Back in the rocks a ways."

"I thought we was in a goddamned rush," Jim said.

"Time now to go slow," Moses cautioned.

"We still don't know if the women are down there."

"That's right," Pete said, looking at Jim. "Why don't you think before you talk?"

"I keep tryin' but it don't come out too good."

They moved back and made a nest for themselves, stretching out on some rocks that were no balm for sore muscles, no comfort against the desert cold that would find them chilled and aching before dawn.

It was a miserable night, of fitful sleep, uncomfortable almost beyond endurance. They spent half of it stirring around, trying to exercise to battle the cold.

Before dawn they ate hard biscuits and tough dried meat and drank from their canteens.

"The way I figure it," Moses said, "we've got one chance to get the women out of that camp and through the front door."

"You won't get a mile down that canyon before you're caught," Jim Ketchel said.

"Not if we seal up the slot," Moses said.

Pete and Jim stared, then Pete tapped his head with his finger and made a wry, wise face. "You see, Jim? Thinking all the time."

"I figure we can make a bomb out of one of the canteens," Moses explained. "Two canteens will hold all the water we have

210

left, but it'll take most of our cartridges to supply the powder. Wedge that in a crack in the rocks, light it when the time comes, and we'll close the door."

"How about the back one?" Jim asked.

"A rock slide," Moses said.

"There you go again," Pete said. "Ain't you ever goin' to learn?" He leaned back and laughed. "Now tell me how you figure out for us to be in three places at one time, Joe."

"Jim, you'll take care of the explosion on the other rim. Pete, you start the slide when the camp gets into an uproar, but after the explosion seals off the canyon. And Jim, you make sure I get clear with the women."

"You're goin' in alone?" Jim said. "You're a damned fool. You'll never make it."

"There's no other way," Moses said. "I'll make the bomb. You two give me your cartridges and then start setting rocks for the slide." He took off his canvas shell belt and dumped the shotgun shells on the ground. "Tonight, late, or maybe just before dawn, we'll make our move."

"You don't even know the women are down there," Pete said.

"There's women down there," Moses

assured him. "There always are in an Apache camp. I'll go in before midnight and scout around, and if I find them, I'll bide my time the best I can and make the escape just before dawn. You'll need some light to see what's going on."

"Damn, that's cutting it fine," Pete said.

"Sure, but what else can we do?" Moses asked.

The sun was a welcome, warming thing after a half-frozen night in the open with no blankets or shelter. Joe Moses spent hours carefully pulling bullets and shot from the cartridges; he could not afford to spill any of the black powder. He used the smallest canteen, something over a quart in size, and partially filled it with clean sand to give it ballast and take up space, then he packed it with powder, right up to the lip of the neck.

Jim and Pete Ketchel carefully piled rocks into a teetery mass that could be easily levered over the rim and cause a devastating slide, one that would wipe out the precarious trail to the rim.

That evening Moses carefully explained to Jim how the charge would have to be set and touched off. The canteen would have to be wedged on its side between two large, loose rocks, so that the open neck was on ground level and dribbling a little powder. The fuse would be a thin, unbroken streak of powder perhaps twenty-five feet long. Moses calculated that this would burn at a foot a second, but they could spare no more powder to make it larger. Jim would barely have time enough to dash back and be clear of the big boom.

Jim Ketchel understood what he had to do and before it got dark he worked his way around to the other side to plant the explosive. They had agreed to meet the following day, if everything went well, five miles down the canyon. Jim shook hands with Moses and left, not sure he was doing the right thing by leaving Moses to take all the risks.

He searched until he found a fissure in which to wedge the canteen; it was almost completely dark and he wondered if Moses had reached the canyon floor yet.

A cool breeze sprang up and when he began to lay the powder train he found that the grains of powder were easily blown away. He wasted a little, then stopped laying it and sat down to think it over. Damn it anyway!

He knew he couldn't wait too long to do the job because he had no way of knowing just when Moses was going to make his break with the women. There wouldn't be time then; he'd have to have it ready to light and, once lit, he'd have to get the hell out of there.

Putting the powder train down in the darkness was slow business; he had to lay his forefinger along the ground and gently pour the powder and do it all by feel and the damned breeze kept blowing it away.

After two tries he knew he didn't have enough powder for twenty-five feet; he'd wasted at least four trying to beat the wind.

What a hell of a mess for a man to be in, he thought as he sat there and tried to figure out what to do. He wished he had Pete's advice. Pete would figure out something; he was always full of ideas and Jim had slipped into the habit of just tagging along. He didn't mind it though because he got along with Pete and he knew a lot of men who couldn't say that about their brothers.

Jim Ketchel bellied down and watched the cook fires. Moses was down there somewhere, watching and waiting. Jim knew it was tougher being down there and he felt ashamed of himself, letting his little troubles push everything else aside this way.

It occurred to him that maybe he could work his way around to the other side and ask Pete what he should do about the powder and the wind; then he figured that with his luck he'd get halfway around and Moses would make his move. So he stayed and stewed about the wind and worried.

One by one the cook fires went out, dying to red nubbins of brightness. The Indian camp was very quiet, the only sounds coming up were from the restless horse herd.

Jim Ketchel didn't know what time it was; he didn't own a watch. But it was late. The moon had come and gone and the wind had picked up if anything; it husked sand and dust along the rim and kept reminding him that time was passing and he hadn't figured anything out yet.

It might have helped if he had known what was going on down below, but he didn't. Moses was there, moving as quiet as a shadow, taking all the risks, and Jim didn't like to think of how Moses would die if he were caught.

It was a terrible thing this waiting, hour after hour, with nothing but the whisper of the wind. He stretched out on one of the rocks that held the canteen of powder captive, his rifle in one hand, chin resting on the other.

Then he heard a sound, a man's cry of alarm, and a grunt as though a blow had been struck. It was completely dark down there, like a pit of mud and he could see nothing. Then there was another sound, a woman's sharp cry of pain as though she had fallen, and it was an alarm bell, a fire gong in the Apache camp. It came alive with a confused roar and men ran around and someone threw wood on the near-dead fires to stoke up a little light.

Near the mouth of the canyon, Joe Moses' shotgun bellowed, coughing a bloom of muzzle flame; then Moses fired the other barrel and Jim Ketchel knew that he had made it through the neck of the draw.

The Apaches were getting their weapons and horses and, Jesus God, he was sitting there on his dumb ass not ready to do anything. Now was the time to do it, and now he knew what he was going to have to do. It hurt like hell because he was rich now and all the years of working his ass off had paid off, but none of it was going to do him any good.

He stood up and waited, waited for the Apaches to get their damned horses and start for the neck of the draw. When they came on, he pressed the muzzle of the rifle right into the neck of the canteen and said,

"I'm thinkin' now, Pete."

Then he squeezed the trigger and the earth mushroomed and rocks roared down, trapping the Apaches, killing many and catching a few more as they approached the pass.

The explosion blocked it completely, piling rubble on rubble, and sending up rank clouds of blinding, choking dust.

Joe Moses was three hundred yards down the draw with the women, running as fast as he could, cursing, pushing them on when they wanted to stop and rest. The ground trembled when the explosion cascaded the rocks down and dust gagged him and small, flying pieces of stone hit him and cut him, but he kept pushing them on until Mrs. Calvin fell. Then he stopped, his breath sawing painfully in his chest.

Pete would start his rock slide now and it would take the Apaches a while to clear a way out, maybe a day, and that would give them time to cover their tracks and put some distance between themselves and the Apaches.

The two women were dressed in rags, barefoot, dazed, relieved, crying, nearly helpless now; he couldn't blame them, for they were free of the Apaches and believed that they were safe, that it was all over — while the truth of it was that they were not safe at all and wouldn't be until they reached Camp Bowie.

Moses let them rest for ten minutes, then said, "We've got to go on, ladies."

Mrs. Calvin looked at him. "How can we? We're used up."

"Ladies, we've got to go on. *I'm* going on. If you want to sit here, then go ahead." He turned and walked on and they followed him, crying, appealing to him, but he paid not the slightest attention to them.

It was near dawn when he reached the rendezvous and found Pete Ketchel waiting. The women collapsed on the ground and rubbed their aching legs.

"Where's Jim?" Moses asked.

"Don't know," Pete said, his worry showing. "He had time to get here. And he wouldn't have missed the place. Not Jim. He could find his way across a desert on a cloudy day." He looked at Moses. "How long can we wait, Joe?"

"Not more than an hour. It'll be daylight soon and we'll have to move on."

Mrs. Calvin roused at this. "Move? We've got to rest. Do you understand? We've got to rest."

Pete Ketchel spelled it out for her very

simply. "You want to die here, ma'am?" He waited for his answer and got none. "All right, then we do like Joe said." His glance touched Moses again. "I wish to God he'd get here. I sure do wish that, Joe."

When the heat became heavy, Joe Moses searched out a high place that was hidden from view on three sides and made camp. He figured they were a good twenty miles from the Apache camp and, although that distance was considerable, it was not half far enough to suit Moses.

Yet he knew they could not go any farther; the women were dead beat, and the young one was so far gone she didn't know where she was.

A fire would have been good, to make coffee — if they'd had any coffee to make; as it was they ate cold rations and washed them down with blood-warm water already growing stale in the canteens.

The women slept and Moses tried to. Pete Ketchel kept watching the land, looking for his brother and knowing it was no use at all.

Finally he said, "I guess he's really gone, Joe," and went to sleep.

When the sun went down and the heat began to disappear, Moses woke, got up and stamped some of the stiffness from his legs. Hunger was a gnawing ache in his stomach and he figured on being eight or ten pounds leaner by the time they reached Bowie. That would be tomorrow night, with luck, and if Moss Railey would spare them horses. The women could stay there, rest up, and he'd send an ambulance and a detail for them.

He hated to do it, but they had to be moving; he gently shook Mrs. Calvin awake and she sat up suddenly, fear large in her eyes. Then she remembered where she was and calmed herself.

"We've got to go on," Moses said. The sound of his voice woke Pete Ketchel who got up and started moving around, swinging his arms.

Mrs. Calvin tried to get up, but she was too sore to do it without help. Moses gave her a hand and she groaned softly.

"I can't stand much more," she said, appealing to him.

"Do you want to go back to the Apaches?" He turned from her and pulled the girl to her feet, shaking her to make her open her eyes. He put his arm around her, supported her, then Pete Ketchel handed him the empty shotgun and they started off, striking out toward Moss Railey's ranch.

He felt sorry for the girl. A bad thing had happened, but it would pass, although he didn't expect her to see that, not now and maybe not ever. A man taken by the Apaches was a dead man, and a woman — well, if she lived, she was never the same again.

Moses had thought about these things when he'd made his way into the Apache camp, found them and got them out. Even then he knew that in the end it might have been kinder to have turned around and left them there with their own form of death, but they were white women and a man just couldn't forget that. He did what was expected of him and afterward he'd have to go on telling himself that it was the right thing, even if it wasn't.

He'd known of a few women brought back. Some had killed themselves, some had tried to pick up some kind of a life and some had just disappeared, losing themselves and the past, or trying to anyway.

He had begun to think they'd never reach Moss Railey's place, when they topped the rim of his valley and started down. When they were two miles away from the buildings, Pete emptied his rifle into the air and then sat down on a rock as though he meant to spend the rest of his life there, just sitting and resting. The women were not capable of sitting; they stretched out in cramped, awkward positions, not caring much about anything now.

Joe Moses watched the Railey place and saw the old man and two of his boys come out; he waved and then saw the boys run for the corral and get horses. It wasn't long before they were riding toward them.

They came up the incline, the horses blowing and pawing for purchase. Moss Railey was the first to fling off. "Jesus God," he said, "what happened?" He made a swinging, cutting motion with his hand when he saw the women. "Asa, go back and get a wagon load of hay. We'll get them down to the valley. Tell the women to make rooms ready."

Asa nodded and rode back, not sparing the horse. Railey looked at Moses a moment, then at Pete Ketchel. "Ain't you — Pete, I didn't know you there at first, used up the way you are. You two raid the Apaches' camp?"

"Jim was with us," Moses said. "He never showed up afterward."

"God," Railey said. He motioned for his son to get down. "Harry, help the women to the horses. Gentle there, boy." He pulled Mrs. Calvin to her feet, stared at her out of curiosity, then shook his head, helped her on the horse and swung up behind her. Harry was trying to get June Stanley to stand and having a time of it and Moses helped him get her up on the horse.

Moss Railey said, "I'll come back for —"

"We're all right," Pete said. "We'll just stagger along." He managed a smile. "If you've got a gallon of coffee, I'd sure —"

"Anything you want, boy," Railey said, his voice a little choked. Then he turned and started down the slope, taking it carefully. Joe Moses unscrewed the cap on his canteen and drank with a great thirst, then he handed it to Pete Ketchel, who finished it.

They sat there for a time and saw Asa come with the wagon and take the women on to the house. Moss Railey came back, leading the horses.

When Pete stepped into the saddle, he grunted from the unusual effort. "Seems like I've been walkin' so long I've forgot how to ride," he said.

Railey hurried back to the ranch but Moses and Ketchel took their time; there was no hurry now. When they reached Railey's yard they swung down by the watering trough. One of the young girls came out with a tray with coffee on it and some soap and towels and a razor.

"Now, if you ain't the sweetest thing," Pete said and took off his shirt. She stood there, holding the tray, not knowing whether to set it down and go back or stand there and watch a strange man strip to the waist.

Moses took it from her and said, "Go on back to the house. And thank you."

Pete washed and shaved and drank his coffee; there was a sack of tobacco and papers under the towel and he rolled a smoke and sat on the edge of the well curbing while Moses shaved.

"Now, that's what I call considerate people," Ketchel said.

The Railey boys made several trips to the well, carrying buckets of water to the house. Moses said, "Ain't one of you missing?"

"Skinny," Asa said, working the pump handle. "He took the captain to Bowie and ain't back yet." He picked up the full buckets. "Pa says to come in, there's a meal on the table."

"All right," Moses said.

They followed Asa to the house where two of Railey's girls were setting platters on the table, bacon and eggs and a stack of wheat cakes. Pete rubbed his hands together as he sat down. "Where does a man start on such a meal? I reckon I'll eat everythin' in sight."

"There's more if you want it," Asa said. "I got to take this water in. Women sure use a lot of it to bathe."

After they had eaten all they could hold, Moss Railey came in, his pipe firmly held in his teeth. "With the women takin' up the spare room, I'll have to put you in the bunk-house. Sorry about that but —"

"Don't apologize," Moses said. "The ground would suit me fine as long as there was some grass on it." He got up and made a cigarette. "The best meal I can remember, Moss. I'll get a few hours' rest and if you'll loan me a horse, I'll ride on to Bowie and have them send an ambulance and detail back for the women."

"I wouldn't have a horse to spare until day after tomorrow," Railey said frankly.

Moses looked at him. "What the hell now, you've got a dozen in your corral."

"This is my place; I run it," the old man said. "I run the people who live on it. Between now and day after tomorrow you're goin' to lay around and eat and sleep and do nothin'. You're as near used up as I've seen a man. Both of you."

"I won't fight you," Pete Ketchel said, smiling.

"Well, I'm in the army and —"

"And you can just forget it until day after tomorrow," Railey put in. "Now, I don't want to hear any more about it. You do as I say or the boys will tie you up."

"All right," Moses said wearily. "I'm too tired to fight about it, Moss."

"Figured you were," he said.

They went to the bunkhouse; it was clean and the straw ticks on the bunks had no lice. Moses took off his boots, stripped to his underwear and stretched out; he sighed and closed his eyes and a moment later he was gently snoring.

Pete finished his cigarette, threw it out the open door, then took off his boots. He sat on the edge of the bunk with one in his hand and his eyes were vacant as though he viewed a faraway place; then he gently put the boot down, curled up and went to sleep.

Moses woke well after dark; he went out and saw lights on in the house and when he approached the porch he found Moss Railey sitting there.

"There's supper in there for you. Trudy's keeping it warm." He nudged a chair around. "Sit a spell."

"How are the women?"

"Resting," Railey said. "I don't know about the young one. She's had the worst of it. Young that way." He shrugged. "But young or old, it would be hell, wouldn't it?"

The youngest Railey girl came out with a plate and a cup of coffee. "Why, thank you," Moses said and smiled at her.

"She's shy," Railey said. "You're a good girl, Trudy. Go back and tend your chores now." He watched Moses eat his stew, then said, "Saw smoke this afternoon. To the north and west. Maybe you stirred up something."

"Maybe," Moses said. "But that wasn't a big camp. My guess was they were renegades who broke away from Cochise or the reservation. At any rate, they lost at least half their number when we blew up the pass."

"Blew up the pass?"

Moses explained quickly how they had rescued the women. When he finished, Railey said, "You just went in and got 'em? That easy, huh?"

"Do you pull the shades down when you undress for bed?"

"Huh? Hell no. Who's to see me?"

"That's the way the Apaches felt," Moses said. "Their camp was well hidden but I just watched until I saw the women working. After I spotted their hogan, it wasn't too hard to get 'em out."

"Havin' done some Apache fightin', I'll just take that with a grain of salt," Railey said, scratching a match to light his pipe. "That smoke worries me though, Moses. Smoke's always meant trouble to me. But I never seen it so far north. Sure would be nice if a man knew what was goin' on."

"I could find out if you let me leave in the morning," Moses said.

"You just can't get an idea out of your head, can you?"

"A man knows what he has to do. You've got a fast horse, Moss. Do it my way this time."

Railey thought about it. "You can take Asa's bay; there ain't a pony in the country that can touch him for speed or stayin' power. I noticed your shell belt's empty, but I've got some eight-gauge brass cases. Double-00 buckshot."

"If I get out around dawn, I can make Tucson by midnight."

"Be quicker to go to Bowie."

Moses shook his head. "I'll go to Tucson."

"You're makin' the ride," Railey said and got up. "Gettin' my bedtime. I'll tell Asa to have the horse and things ready. You want your army saddle?"

Moses nodded.

Railey stopped in the doorway. "About that captain — he wasn't the one, Joe."

"I'll be damned. I thought he was. Did your girl say?"

"Yes. Baker. He was here with Dane. I'll have to see him about this. He ain't married, is he?"

"No, he's still single," Moses said. "Don't you have enough trouble, Moss?"

Railey shrugged. "What man doesn't? But that never keeps him from askin' for more, does it?"

"I guess not," Moses said and drank his coffee before it got cold.

Before dawn he met Asa at the barn; he had a small sack of food for Moses, and the canvas shell belt was full again. Moses looked the horse over, a leggy gelding with a big chest and a proud, arched nose.

"Be a shame to throw a saddle on him," Moses said.

"He likes to go," Asa said. "You get into trouble, just give him his head and set yourself for a ride."

"I'll ride him bareback," Moses said.

"He likes that," Asa said.

Moses flipped up and turned the horse out of the barn. "I'll take good care of him, Asa."

"Do, 'cause money can't buy him."

The sky was a faint gray when Moses rode out, heading southwest. The bay was full of hell, wanting to stretch out and run; Moses let him go for better than a mile, then pulled him down to an easy trot.

In the early morning he saw smoke in four places and he couldn't read it; he knew of only two white men who could, but Indian smoke meant trouble, even without a literal translation.

Twice he stopped to rest the horse, and twice he walked the bay for almost a mile. In the late afternoon, to save time, he crossed a broad sandy valley floor. Far off to the right he saw dust and knew that it was made by Apache ponies.

The distance was three miles, which was close enough, so he let the bay run. The last time he looked back he saw that the Apaches had given up, turned back, lost interest, and it suited him fine.

When it got dark he was in the mountains again, threading along a high pass. He ate as he moved, cold meat and biscuits, and afterward drank from his canteen.

The bay was getting tired, and Moses was tired, yet he had a far piece to go and time was passing away. All Moses could do was to urge the horse on while mentally promising him the fullest grain bag and the best rubdown in Tucson when they got there.

The guard at Camp Lowell's main gate was sleepy and Joe Moses was almost upon him before he realized he was there; the soldier came alert, his carbine ready. He let Moses come on, until the light from the hanging lanterns touched him, then the soldier said, "That's far enough! State your business."

"Sergeant Moses. Open the damned gate."

The soldier peered closer, then laughed. "I sure as hell didn't expect you." He stepped back and swung half the gate wide so Moses could pass through.

"What's the idea of keeping the gate closed?" Moses asked.

"Why, this is war!" the soldier said. "Ain't you heard?"

"I haven't heard anything but the wind," Moses said and walked the horse across the parade ground. The hour was late but the post seemed oddly deserted; Moses swung down, tied up, stepped across the porch and went into the orderlies' room. A lone corporal looked around. He sat in a tilted-back chair and when he saw Moses his feet and the chair legs thumped the floor together and he rushed into the commander's office.

"Lieutenant Bishop, sir — Moses is back!"

Bishop came out and had a look for himself; he was a short, stocky man with a wrestler's shoulders and short, powerful legs. "Come in, Sergeant. Corporal, see to the sergeant's horse."

"I borrowed him," Moses said. "See that he gets a good rub and some oats."

"There's no one at the stable," the corporal said.

"Then put him in a stall and throw a blanket over him," Moses said. "Where the hell is everybody?"

"Come on inside, Sergeant," Bishop said, closing the door after him. "Sit down. Drink? Cigar?"

"Both," Moses said. Bishop poured a glass and gave him a cigar and a light.

"Captain Dane returned to the post," Bishop said. "He reported that you went on alone. That was pretty foolish, Sergeant."

"I didn't have a choice, sir," Moses said. He tossed off the drink then wiped his watering eyes. "I'll be glad when the old man makes colonel so he can buy some decent stuff. You didn't say, sir, where everyone —"

Bishop turned to a wall map. "A detail from Lieutenant Travis sent us the news of the tragedy. Major Hargus, with three companies, left day before yesterday, sweeping northeast. He left a skeleton force of twenty men at Fort Thomas. From Camp Apache, Captain Leverson and two companies are pushing southeast, while Captain Rainey moves east from Grant with three companies. Major Fickland and the entire command has joined Rainey." He made a circling motion with his finger. "By tomorrow morning they'll have Cochise blocked off somewhere in there, along the south fork of the Gila." He turned and sat down. "The country is in an uproar, Moses. We hope, somehow, to retake the women."

"They're at Railey's ranch," Moses said.

Bishop looked up. "I beg your pardon?"

Moses repeated it, then gave Bishop a terse, accurate account of the rescue. When he was through, Bishop put a hand to his face and shook his head.

"Now I understand what all the smoke was about," Moses said. "There's going to be some dying out there tomorrow, sir. I don't think Mrs. Calvin and her niece would want to be the cause of it."

"None of it was our decision anyway," Bishop said. "Or maybe it was a decision that just had to be made because no one ever wanted peace with the Apaches anyway. No one would have trusted them if they swore on a stack of Bibles." He sighed and leaned back in his chair. "I've got twenty-five men on the post. How am I going to send an ambulance and escort to Railey's ranch?"

"If I could get ten or twelve hours' sleep —"

"To hell with that," Bishop said quickly. "I'll work something out." He pushed the bottle across the desk. "Take that along with you if you want."

Moses shook his head. "I'm a one-drink man, Lieutenant. Thanks just the same."

He left the office, went to the stable and spent thirty minutes rubbing down the bay; then he put a clean, dry blanket over him, checked the feed box and unhooked the lantern from the harness peg. He stepped to the door and was almost there when he saw someone standing in the shadows.

Mildred Dane said, "Joe," stepped up to him and into his arms, her mouth warm and wet against his. He held her for a long moment, stroking her hair, then he gently pushed her back so he could look at her.

"How did you know —"

She shook her head. "I don't know. I just knew. Maybe it's because I've slept with both ears listening, with every nerve waiting."

He put his arm around her and blew out the lantern. "You wouldn't have any coffee, would you?"

"Yes. Anything you want."

He thought about that. "Isn't that a broad subject?"

"It is."

They started walking back. "Well, maybe the coffee and I'll hold your hand now and then."

"That doesn't satisfy me now," she said. "I just had to tell you that straight out."

"Did you see George when he came back?"

"No," she said quickly. "I heard he'd been beaten. Did you do it?"

"A sergeant doesn't strike an officer," Moses said. "The Railey bunch did it. It was a mistake."

"You may think so," Mildred said, "but I just can't think of it as anything but wholly deserving. I hate him, Joe."

"Hate and love are not far —"

"Now, don't say that," she said. They reached her quarters; he opened the door for her, then closed it after they stepped inside. A lamp was turned down on the table and she took it and they went into the kitchen where she stoked the fire and put on the coffeepot.

"I went into town yesterday," she said.

"Shopping?"

She shook her head. "I saw a lawyer, the same one George hired to file for a divorce. We had a nice chat. I told him that I wanted to sue for divorce and that the boys were mine and I meant to fight for them. He listened very attentively. I convinced him that it was one thing to file for an uncontested divorce when I was two thousand miles away, and quite another when I was here to raise all kinds of hell. That made sense to him. Besides, he'd already been paid a fee by George, and adding mine to that — well, the profits added up and he was very nice about it all."

"You're not fooling me," Moses said. "It's a rotten business and you know it."

She looked at him a moment, then came over and sat on his lap and put her arms around him. "I know it is. I think that's just as bad as — well, just bad." She patted his cheek and got up to pull the coffeepot off the hot spot on the stove. Then she got out a skillet. "All I have is bacon and eggs."

"Don't go to the —"

She turned her head quickly and looked at him. "Joe, don't say it."

He shrugged and smiled. "All right. I won't even think it, then." He scraped a hand across his scratchy beard stubble. "A man ought to shave before he calls on a pretty woman. I like your hair. You know that? And you've got nice eyes. Want me to go on?"

"Is there more?"

He laughed. "I was just starting at the top and —"

"Maybe you'd better stop," she said.

She sat across from him while he ate. He asked her about the boys and was surprised to know that they lived with her; she explained how it had happened.

"Well," he said, "that was a mistake on my part. I figured that any woman who'd marry George Dane was as selfish as he was."

"She really loved the boys," Mildred said. "I'm sure of it." She got up to get him some bread and sat down again. "I wish I knew how to thank her, Joe."

"She didn't do it for thanks."

He wiped his plate clean and had another cup of coffee, then got up and stretched to ease the soreness in his back.

"I don't want you to go," she said. "I've been sitting here wondering how I could keep you from going."

"We've got to do what's right," Moses said. "You know that."

He kissed her and she went to the door with him. "See me tomorrow."

"Sure," he said and went out, crossing to his dark quarters.

He slept late, then went to headquarters and found Lieutenant Bishop in his office. The orderly was out so Moses knocked and went in. Bishop said, "Well, your eyes are red, but I think you'll live. What's on your mind, Sergeant?"

"The Calvin woman and her niece," Moses said.

"We'll get them, we'll get them," Bishop said. "But in good time." He held up one finger. "There's one officer on the post besides me — Lieutenant Malcolm Baker — and he's in town and won't be back until late this afternoon. Now, you don't expect me to turn the post over to him while I go after the Calvin woman, do you?"

Moses showed his surprise. "I thought Baker resigned."

"He put in his letter but this whole thing held it up."

"And Nora Frazer, the girl who came out to —"

Bishop shook his head. "Kind of bad business there, Moses. I tell you because you'll hear about it anyway and you might as well get it straight. You might say they've made plans. She moved to the hotel in town and Baker spends a lot of time there."

"Daytime, sir?"

Bishop shook his head. "It's a bad thing. God damn it, an officer ought to marry a woman before he sleeps with her. He's got a certain reputation to maintain."

"Sir, I'd like permission to convince Mr. Baker that he should go to Railey's with a detail. Just four men, myself, Baker, and an ambulance."

"If you can convince Baker, I'll authorize it," Bishop said.

"Thank you, sir," Moses said and went out.

He got a horse from the stable, saddled and rode to Tucson, knowing what he had to do and not liking it any. The town was crowded; the Indian-army trouble had brought a lot of the ranchers and their families into town where it was safe. No one thought that the Apaches would attack the town — at least, they hadn't yet.

Moses was tying up in front of the hotel when Al Roan, the marshal, came down the walk. "Joe! Hold up there." He trotted up. "O. B. Calvin wants to see you."

"Can't it wait, Al?"

"Hell, the man just heard this morning," Roan said. "Bishop sent a soldier in with the news. O.B. just broke down and cried in front of everybody. Come on. Talk to him. Whatever the rush is, it can wait that long."

Moses hesitated, then shrugged and followed Roan across the traffic-clogged street. Calvin's saloon was crowded as they pushed through to the back room; Roan knocked, then stepped inside.

When Calvin saw Moses, he stopped writing in his account book and slowly got up and came around his desk. He took Moses' hand as though he never meant to let go of it.

"What does a man say at a time like this, Moses?"

"Nothing to say, I guess. I was glad to get them out."

"Sit down. Roan, tell the bartender to bring a good bottle in here. And some of those Havana cigars." He sat on the edge of his desk and looked at Moses. "I broke down when I heard. When the news from Travis came in, it hit me harder than anything in my life. You've got to believe that, Moses."

"I believe it, and like I said, I'm glad they're both safe now. But they had a tough time. You know."

Calvin nodded and Al Roan came back with bottle and glasses and a box of cigars under his arm. He poured three and they drank and Calvin passed around the cigars, shoving a fistful into Moses' shirt pocket.

"I've got to say this, Moses; my conscience will never let me rest until I do. You've been an ache to me."

"What the hell did I ever do to you?" Moses asked.

"George Dane and I made some pretty elaborate plans and you always messed them up somehow." He saw Moses' frown and laughed. "Dane found silver, you know. A rich one. We wanted our share, and everybody else's for that matter. Between the two of us, we were going to make a big operation of it, but it took money and Dane didn't have much. He's a schemin' bastard, you know. Couldn't go out and stick up a bank like a man. Naw, he had to figure out a way to marry it." Calvin shook his head. "We should have went in there alone and fought for it. The trouble is, we both wanted it the easy way."

"Well, you both missed it," Moses said. "Jim and Pete Ketchel staked it."

O. B. Calvin stared for a minute, then tipped back his head and roared with laughter. He laughed until tears rolled down his cheeks.

"Is it that funny?" Al Roan asked.

"It's hilarious," Calvin said, calming himself. He wiped his eyes and poured a drink. "I don't mind getting left with the bag, Moses. It's like I told Dane once, it's all money I haven't got, so I don't worry too much about it. But *you* want a favor from me and you've just got to ask it. Not just one. Any time, as long as I live." He wiped his eyes. "I love that woman, Moses. She's stood by me when times were thin and people wouldn't speak to her because she was married to a saloon keeper. You want a favor, you just ask."

"You can tell me where I'll find Lieutenant Baker."

"In the hotel, ruttin' that girl," Calvin said bluntly. "Someone ought to kick the hell out of him. She's a nice girl and he'll get her in trouble."

"I'll go get Baker," Roan said, turning to the door.

"Don't kick the hell out of him," Moses warned. "I may want to do it."

"You can use my back storeroom," Calvin said generously. After Al Roan went out, Calvin leaned back and closed his eyes. "This Indian trouble popped suddenly, didn't it?"

"It was building up," Moses said. "And it won't be over tomorrow either. Some of these commanders think they'll run the Apaches into a hole and that'll be the end of it. But this may go on for four or five years."

"Will this country ever be worth a good goddamn?"

Moses shrugged. "It's worth fighting over, isn't it? The Indians think so and the army thinks so and the Washington politicians think so because they keep appropriating the money to build up the posts out here."

"I hear all kinds of rumors out here," Calvin said. "The latest is that they're sending a general — Crook's his name — to get this whole thing organized."

"I've heard of him. Old iron ass himself," Moses said. He jerked around in his chair as the door was flung open and Malcolm Baker was propelled into the office ahead of Al Roan.

"What the hell, am I under arrest or

something?" he asked. Then he saw Moses and he stared. "What are you doing here, Sergeant?"

"Waiting for you, sir. We're going back to the post."

"That's what you think."

"Lieutenant Bishop's orders, sir."

"Tell Bishop you couldn't find me."

"I've already found you," Moses said.

Al Roan said, "Why don't you mind the sergeant like a good boy, sonny?"

"What the hell's this to you?" Baker snapped. "You're in the army, Sergeant. When I give you an order, you jump."

"Not in here," Calvin told him.

"We're going to the Railey ranch with an ambulance and a detail," Joe Moses said and watched concern come into Baker's face. "And while you're there, Mr. Baker, you're going to hold that pregnant girl's hand in front of a lot of witnesses and marry her and the old man will record it in the family Bible."

Baker suddenly wheeled, trying to make the door, but Al Roan blocked him. He would have knocked Baker back with his fist had not Moses spoken sharply: "Don't hit him!"

Moses toed a chair around. "Sit down, sir."

"Better do as he says," Calvin suggested tightly. "If you get cocky and someone has to beat some decency into you, we'll swear some stranger did it. Now sit down."

When Baker lowered himself in the chair, Moses sat on the corner of the desk and looked at him steadily. "You're not a very strong man, sir, but maybe there's enough decency in you to make up for it. Back east Nora Frazer looked good to you and you made some damned foolish promises to her. Then you came back and the Railey girl looked good and she let you have your fool's way with her. All right, Mr. Baker, she got caught. Now you've got to do something about it." He reached out and tapped Baker on the chest with his finger. "You've got to tell Nora Frazer that it's been nice, but this is good-bye."

"God! I can't! Not now," Baker said. He looked at Roan and O. B. Calvin and saw only hardness in their faces and no understanding at all. "Why are you doing this to me? What's it to you? You tell me that, huh?"

Calvin said, "I don't know. Maybe it's that there's so little real good out here that I want to preserve what we have." He got up from his desk. "We can see that you don't have the guts to face the Frazer girl, o sit down and write her a letter. Go on, t's your easiest way out. And tell her the ruth." He picked up the pen, dipped it in he inkwell and handed it to Baker, who ook it and held it as though he couldn't hink of what to say.

Al Roan said, "Joe, why don't you go back to the post? I'll see that Mr. Baker gets there, after he finishes up here."

"You do that, Joe," Calvin urged. "Al and I are not in the army and if we have to talk harshly to Mr. Baker, we don't have any stripes to lose."

"There are things I should be doing," Moses admitted. "Mr. Baker's got to ride tomorrow. I hope you remember that."

"He'll be able to ride," Roan promised.

Joe Moses went out through the crowded saloon and across to his horse. He started to mount up, then changed his mind and went into the hotel. The clerk gave him the number of Nora Frazer's room and he walked down a narrow hallway, knocked, and heard her step.

She was expecting Baker; he could tell from the expression on her face.

"Oh, it's you. What do you want?"

He looked at her carefully; she wore a dressing robe and he supposed little else. Her hair was loose around her shoulders, as though she had just got up from the bed, and her eyes seemed more tired, older than he remembered.

"I just wanted to see you," he said. "Don't know why."

"Well, now that you've seen me, get the hell out of here." She started to close the door, but he put out his hand and stopped her.

"I'd like to come in for a minute, if you don't mind."

"Would it make any difference if I did?" She stepped aside and he closed the door.

"I'd like to know, Miss Frazer, if you finally got what you came here for?"

"I suppose I got all I'm going to get," she said. "Do you care?"

"Not now," he said and opened the door. "Sorry to have bothered you."

"No bother," she said, then laughed.

"Is something funny?"

"You," she said. "You just can't help sticking your nose in someone else's business, can you?"

"I should have left you in Lordsburg."

"But you didn't," she said. "Sergeant why don't you go fight the Indians or do something useful?"

"Good idea," he said and closed the door.

When he had mounted his horse and turned toward the post he felt better. She was no longer a cause for worry to him because he knew she could take care of herself. It was a thing she had learned between the trip from Lordsburg and the hotel room, and he wasn't sure it was a good thing for a woman to know.

Moses spent part of the day carefully selecting horses and checking equipment. Lieutenant Bishop offered him his choice of any four men left on the post; they all wanted to go, but Moses made his selection; a corporal from the commander's office, a cook from the mess hall, and two men just released from the stockade. He chose them because they were tough and had fought the Apaches before and lived to learn something from it.

The ambulance was greased and all the spokes checked; the wheels were soaked in water to tighten the wood and the bolts were gone over with a spanner and the harness minutely inspected.

Late in the afternoon, Al Roan came from town with Lieutenant Baker, who surprised Moses by riding upright in the saddle. Roan brought him right onto the post and on to the stable yard where Moses waited.

Roan crossed his hands on the saddle horn and said, "Mr. Baker's done the decent thing, Joe. It wasn't so bad now, was ft, Mr. Baker?" He waited for Baker to speak, and when he didn't, Roan went on. "You got to give him credit, Joe; he told her to her face. Two drinks and he walked across that street and told her to her face. She belted him a couple of times in the chops and called him some choice but fittin' names, and that was that. I keep tellin' him that he's lucky to get rid of her. I've seen 'em turn hard and there's nothin' worse than a hard woman."

"What are you going to do, talk about it the rest of your damned life?" Baker snapped. He swung down and started to hand Moses the reins, then thought better of it and took the horse into the barn.

"He's glad it's over," Roan said.

"How can you tell?"

"Just can. Good luck, Joe." He turned his horse and rode back to town.

Moses waited a moment and went into the barn. Baker was putting his saddle on a tree and hanging the bridle. He looked at Moses and said, "Why don't I hate your damned guts?"

"You tell me."

"Would it bother you if I did?"

"No," Moses said. "You're too light a man to worry about, sir." He leaned his shoulders against the stall. "Good family with money didn't do you much good. It's a shame. I guess it bothers you. No man likes to disappoint others. He likes it even less when he disappoints himself."

"That's right," Baker said. "Moses, I'm not as bad as you think."

"I want to leave before daybreak, and don't tell me that it's your decision," Moses said. He straightened. "When we're off the post, I'll tell you what to do, and you can tell it to the others. It's none of their business —"

"Don't expect me to thank you for that," Baker snapped.

"Shit, man, I never expected anything of you," Moses said and walked to his quarters for some sleep.

Lieutenant Bishop saw him cross the parade ground and knocked as Moses was peeling off his boots. "I see that Baker is back."

"Yes, sir, and rarin' to go."

Bishop smiled. "I won't ask you how you managed that; I've been in the army nine years and right off I learned not to question sergeants too closely. I trust, however, that you've done nothing chargeable."

"Oh, no, sir. Mr. Baker just saw the light. He's going to get married, sir."

"Well, that's something. There's some talk going on in Tucson about Baker and the Frazer girl."

"He's not marrying her, sir. It's the Railey girl. He's got her in a family way."

"Jesus God!" Bishop said. "Doesn't anyone believe in abstinence any more?"

"I don't think it's taught at the Academy, sir."

"Very funny." Bishop took off his kepi and tossed it on a vacant bunk, then sat down. "I wish to hell someone would send back a dispatch. Or send someone to mind the store while I rejoin the command." He sighed, got up and put on his kepi. "I suppose I'd better invite Baker to supper tonight. It's protocol. See if you can persuade Mrs. Dane to move into town. All the other wives did."

"A woman of very independent mind," Moses said. "You talk to her, sir."

"Thank you, no." He smiled and went out and Moses closed his eyes. He knew why Mildred Dane was on the post, because he was there. That was good to know and bad to know, because he was a soldier and she was an officer's wife getting a divorce. The army would never like that and he didn't think many people would really accept it either.

He could get out; there was always that. But she wouldn't want him to give up his life for her; she was like that and he wasn't going to change her, or even try to.

He didn't remember falling asleep, and it was dark when he woke, a kind of thin, predawn darkness. He fished into his pocket for his watch and a match; it was almost four-thirty and he realized he had slept straight through.

In another half hour he'd have to be leaving; he pulled on his boots and hurried across to Mildred Dane's quarters and tapped softly on her door. It opened quickly, as though she had been awake and listening. He stepped inside, putting his arms around her, feeling the firm roundness of her through her cotton nightdress.

"You were sleeping and I didn't have the heart to wake you," she said. "We haven't much time now, have we?"

"Almost none," he said. "I love you, Mildred."

"Yes, and it's so wonderful." Her lips found his and when she pulled back she laughed softly and buried her face in his shoulder. "Come back to me, Joe."

"How could I not?"

When he stepped out, there was a lamp on in headquarters and the detail was waiting with the ambulance. Baker was there, checking arms and ammunition; he nodded when Moses came up, but said nothing.

Ten minutes later they were mounted, flanking the ambulance, driving off the post, Baker and Moses in the lead, with a man on each side of the ambulance, one following, and one man driving.

The first flush of the sun was pink, like rinsed blood. Baker said, "We might pick up some more men at Bowie."

"Don't count on it. Besides, it's the long way."

"You're in a hurry to get there."

"Moss Railey lives to hell and gone away from help when he needs it," Moses said. "If the Apaches try to hit his place, he'll need all the rifles he can get." He turned in the bland light and stared at Baker. "Or do you want to see that girl dead?"

"No," Baker admitted. "Moses, I don't expect you to believe it, but I had a strong feeling for her. Now that I'm going back, I'm glad of it."

"Tell her that when you get there."

Moss Railey and his sons had been keeping an around-the-clock watch since the first smoke, but they saw no Apaches. They were being drawn toward the Gila and Railey suspected that there was some hellish fighting going on there.

He was having his supper when Asa who was on lookout whistled. The old man left the table, picked up his repeater and went outside. Asa was on the roof of the barn and he pointed down the valley. Railey squinted his eyes and made out the ambulance and the escort.

"Well, jumpin' Jesus," he said and laughed. "That's a welcome sight."

"Can I come down now, Pa?"

"Sure, boy. Get your supper. Tell the women to put on some food. They'll be here in a half hour."

He went to his rocking chair and sat there, rocking and watching, and when the detail drew into the yard, went to meet it. He saw Baker and looked steadily at the man. Baker said, "Where is she?"

"In the house," Railey said, nodding.

"Take care of the detail," Baker said to Moses and got down and trotted across the yard.

"That's your new son-in-law," Moses said.

"Is he much of anything?" Railey asked.

"Now, you know I won't answer that,"

Moses told him. He told the detail to put up the horses and the ambulance and he washed at the trough. "Any sign of Indians?"

"None yet," Railey said. "Depends on how the army makes out. If they lick the Indians, then there's no worry. But if they don't, the Apaches will get cocky and they'll hit here. We've been keepin' a close watch."

"We'll stay three or four days," Moses said.

Railey frowned. "Don't the lieutenant give the orders?"

"He listens carefully to me."

"Must be a new kind of army."

"We have an understanding," Moses pointed out.

"That's good. Most men don't. How's that captain?"

"Off fighting Indians."

"I wish him luck," Railey said.

"Why don't you go in and talk to your new son-in-law?"

"You keep sayin' that," Railey mentioned. "Joe, are you pushin' me into somethin' here?"

"Just bringing you what you wanted," Moses said. "And try to remember that the girl picked him, not you."

Moss Railey frowned. "Now you're

talking like a horse trader. Don't know as I really trust you, Joe." He turned toward the house, stopped, looked back, then shrugged and went in.

Moses took his horse to the barn and wondered if it was really possible for any man to do the right thing.

10

There was a stillness to the dawn that gave Joe Moses an uneasy, itching feeling at the back of his neck. Moss Railey felt it too because he had the boys eat in shifts and he came outside to stand with Moses on the porch.

Lieutenant Baker came out, opened his mouth to say something, then thought better of it; he stood there, listening to nothing. Finally Railey spoke: "Not an animal stirring. I don't like that. The world just ain't that quiet." He turned and looked at Baker. "You'll find the loft of the barn is built of solid cottonwood logs with small windows on four sides. My suggestion is that you get your men up there and keep 'em there. You can cover the yard and the house from there."

"Do you think there's a —"

"It's an Apache kind of day, sir," Moses put in.

Baker nodded and trotted across the yard to the barn. Railey and Moses stood there and watched the sky grow progressively lighter.

"I can smell 'em out there," Railey said softly. " 'Course I can't, really, but the feelin's that strong. Let's get inside."

He turned to the door and was starting through when a brass-bellied Sharps buffalo rifle boomed and the fifty-caliber bullet thudded into the frame. Railey dived inside and Moses followed him, slamming the heavy door while bullets hammered into it.

Window glass shattered and in Mrs. Railey's cupboard, glassware settled in broken ruin on the shelf.

"My good plates," Mrs. Railey said and picked up a long-barreled shotgun, her expression determined.

The Apaches came on, yelling, shooting, running across the yard and Baker wisely let them close the range before opening up. Crouched by a window, Moses saw three Indians fall; he knew they would not be stopped, but Baker was cutting into them, costing them men.

He estimated that there were thirty or forty; it was hard to tell. They rushed the house blindly and the devastating fire from repeating rifles did not stop them. One brave buck even hurled himself through a window and was shot dead by Mrs. Railey before he hit her clean kitchen floor.

The Apaches lost nine men and several wounded, and they drew back. The silence fell again, thick and complete. Two of the Railey boys picked up the dead Indian and pitched him outside, out through the window he had shattered.

Moss Railey fed shells into his Spencer. "We're in for a good one, Joe. All day today and maybe tomorrow."

At the south window, Asa said, "Smoke, Pa."

They looked and saw it on a promontory across the valley. Moss Railey gave it some thought. "Yep, a good one this time. They'll have help, come late afternoon." He looked at Joe Moses. "I guess the army didn't do so good after all."

"Looks like," Moses said. He looked around and found Mrs. Railey and the girls methodically cleaning up the broken glass and litter. The pregnant one was down on her hands and knees with a scrub brush washing up the blood.

Mrs. Railey saw Moses watching them and said, "If you think I'm going to meet my Maker with a dirty house, then you've got another think comin', Joseph Moses."

He grinned because he couldn't help it. "Ma'am, you're a long way from the grave."

"Well, I'll be ready just the same."

Moses did not see Mrs. Calvin or her niece so he went into the back of the house and found them in the corner of the back bedroom. The youngest Railey boy was by the window, rifle in hand, a box of cartridges spilled on the floor where they'd be easy to get at.

"Everything all right in front?" he asked.

"Just fine. Some broken glass, that's all."

"More of Ma's dishes," he said, shaking his head. "It sure riles her — more than anything, I guess."

Moses looked at Mrs. Calvin. "You two ladies could help some."

Mrs. Calvin shook her head repeatedly and June Stanley didn't even look around. Moses was not angered by this. He understood there were some things that each person found he just couldn't face. Yet he knew that each had to face them when the time came.

So he put anger and disgust in his voice, and made his words hard and hurting. "What are you going to do, hide whenever someone mentions an Indian? Why don't you crawl under the bed? You can pull the peepot over your head."

His words reached Mrs. Calvin and stung her. She got up and pulled June

Stanley to her feet. She slapped her hard and said, "You heard him. June, stand up!"

"Please, please, Aunt —"

"That's enough of that!" Mrs. Calvin snapped. She pushed the girl ahead of her. "Thank you, Sergeant. We all need reminding now and then of our duties."

The young Railey boy was looking at Moses. "If the young one don't give up, she'll be all right," he said.

"How old are you, Cy?"

"I'm sixteen."

"That's old," Moses said and went out.

Moss Railey turned from his watch. "Nothin' stirrin' out there. They're lickin' their wounds and waitin' for that help to show up." He put down his gun and filled his pipe. Mrs. Calvin and June Stanley were in the kitchen, working at the stove with the oldest Railey girl. "I can't get over the army. I guess us civilians never thought too much of all this ridin' around playin' soldier boy, but we figured that fightin' was one thing they knew how to do right."

"Major Fickland's no fool," Moses said, feeling that he had to defend someone. That was the trouble with the army; the general made a mess and it was handed on down, reflecting on the last private in the rear rank.

"I ain't seen nothin' to the contrary," Railey said.

They sweltered out a day of waiting under a brass sun, and in mid-afternoon they could look out over the valley and see nearly a hundred Apaches gathering. They camped a mile from the Railey ranch and that night their cook fires burned brightly.

"Now, don't that beat all for brazen," Railey said. "Come dawn, they'll rush us like a swarm of ants and we just don't have enough men or guns to hold them off." He was standing by the window, eating his supper; he had the coffee cup on the windowsill and kept reaching for it and rinsing each mouthful down. "They're like cats when they get on the scent, lose all sense except awareness of their game. I can't say I like bein' the game, though."

"I guess that's Cochise," Moses said softly. "Well, I hope there's enough left for the history books to write about."

"Who the hell cares about the history books?" Railey said.

They ate in shifts, each going to the kitchen in turn for their plate. June Stanley was dishing up when Moses got his. He said, "You all right now?"

"As much as I'll ever be," she said, not looking at him.

"Do you know who I am?"

She looked at him then, looked at him for a long time, then shook her head.

This angered Mrs. Calvin. She said, "He's Joe Moses and he came into the Apache camp and got us out."

"Thank you for that," June Stanley said. She was wearing a Railey girl's dress, a cotton dress with sleeves just below the elbow and a fluff of ruffle at the throat. She was quite pretty.

"You're going to be all right," Moses said.

Mrs. Calvin said, "I can hear all the talk. Sergeant, we don't want to be taken again."

Mrs. Railey, who was getting a jar of her preserves from the root cellar, thrust her head up through the opening in the floor and said, "There'll be no suicides around here. And no men shootin' the women either." She crawled out, grunting a little from the effort. "There used to be a family at the far end of the valley. One day a passel of Apaches came to water their horses. The man killed his wife and two small children and then himself to escape torture." She rolled her bony shoulders. "What torture? I ask you. No, there'll be none of it around here." She kicked the trapdoor shut. "My Moss and the boys have thought things out pretty careful; they're clever that way. If the Apaches breach the house, we'll go into the root cellar. There's another trapdoor there, leading to a tunnel that runs a hundred yards on past the barn and corral and comes out in the trees by the creek. There's a couple of tons of rock in there, held up by shoring and a trip board. Once we pass through, we can pull that and seal this end. The Apaches will have a hard time finding the other end because it's been filled in with dirt and it's growed over. There's tools near the far end to dig your way out, and food and water so we can stay a couple of days if we have to." She nodded briskly. "And don't tell me it don't work. We survived one burn-out that way."

"We didn't know about that," June Stanley said meekly.

Mrs. Railey snorted. "Young lady, there's a lot in this world you don't know."

There was Indian medicine being made that night, with dancing and a lot of singing. Everyone had to listen to it because it kept them awake and it was after midnight before the fires began to die and the dancing stopped.

"Got to rest up for tomorrow, I guess," Railey said. "We'll stand guard in shifts anyway, although there ain't much danger. They don't like night fightin'. For that I don't blame 'em." He looked at Moses and grinned. "I ain't much for fightin' of any kind. If I had my way I'd as soon put up my gun and never look at it the rest of my life unless I wanted a little fresh game for the table."

"Someday maybe," Moses said. "But people have been saying that for centuries. When I was in school studying English history I was surprised to find that they fought all the time, either each other or enemies from another country. I never did understand why it was a lot easier for a man to hate someone than to love him."

"Truth there," Railey admitted. "I know —"

The distant blast of a C-horn blowing the charge broke into his soft run of talk. Then the ground throbbed with the drum of running horses and the Apache camp was full of panic and gunfire. Soon the smell of raised dust drifted to the Railey place and they could feel it settle on their faces.

Everyone came out of the house, even Mrs. Calvin and her niece; she clapped her hands and cried and said, "It's the army, it's the army, kill them all, kill every one of them."

Lieutenant Baker came trotting from the barn, pistol in one hand, saber in the other. "By God, I wish I were out there," he said.

Moses looked at him. "Haven't you had enough?" he asked, and knew it was a foolish question for Baker was a man and man never had enough; he simply went on and on until he died or was killed.

In the darkness there was no discerning the turn of the battle, but from the sound of it Moses guessed that at least six companies of cavalry were involved. They had the Indians surrounded, completely cut off.

The battle did not end quickly, and he hadn't expected it to. All night long there was a firecracker popping of small arms and twice the Apaches tried to rush the encircling troops and were pushed back, beaten and mauled back. When dawn came the army had established itself in shallow trenches and had erected a rear area where wagons and tents clustered about and three surgeons worked endlessly over the wounded.

A detachment of five men, Lieutenant Travis leading them, came on to the Railey place. Travis swung down, surprised to find Baker and Joe Moses there.

"Are there any casualties, Sergeant?"

"None, sir."

Travis dismissed his detail to the well and went on into the house with Railey and Joe Moses. They introduced him to Mrs. Calvin and her niece and coffee was served while the popping of small arms fire cut through the silence of the room. Travis drank his coffee and wiped his tired eyes.

"We've covered some miles these last few days," he said. "Major Fickland's command had a brush with the main body night before last; the Apaches killed eleven of his men and vanished, taking this direction. We gathered above Cedar Creek, Captain Rainey, myself, Captain Leverson, and two companies from Major Hargus' command. The major figured they'd hit here. He was right." Travis smiled. "He was also right when he said you'd be able to beat off the first attack."

The firing stopped and its absence startled them for there was a strangeness to it. They got up and went outside and looked out onto the valley toward the center of that stillness. Cavalrymen moved in among the Indians, gathering weapons, herding them into a close knot of confinement.

"They've surrendered," Jefferson Travis

said. "Come along, Sergeant. You stay here, Baker."

They caught up their horses and rode out. By the time they got there, a group of ten Indians was standing before Major Fickland's hastily thrown up command post. They gave their horses to a sentry and went on into this and when Fickland saw Joe Moses he motioned for him to come up and stand by him.

"Which one is Cochise, Moses?"

It felt strange, standing there, looking at those fierce faces, looking at the enemy he had lived with for so many years and had so rarely seen. They were alike, half naked, foul smelling, and he looked at their eyes and pointed.

"He's Cochise."

Fickland nodded, then said, "Bring up the scout so I can talk to him."

"He understands, sir," Moses said.

"Take the others away and keep them together," Fickland said and the guards moved in, leaving Cochise standing alone. Fickland studied the man, then blew out a long breath. "What does he expect now, Sergeant?"

"Death," Moses said without hesitation. "If he were in your place he'd have you all killed." He glanced at Fickland. "Sir, may I offer a comment?"

"Go ahead, Sergeant."

"He expects you to deal harshly with him, sir. There's no word in his language for love or mercy. There is no word for fear either."

"I see," Fickland said. He thought a moment, then looked at Cochise. "I'm going to put you and your people on the reservation. I know you won't stay, that you'll break away. You may as well know something else too: the army will hunt you down again. There will be more fighting until you stay on the reservation." Fickland stood up and stepped up to Cochise. "I give you no word on anything, Cochise. I won't say that the white man will not steal your land because he will. I make no promise to you and I want you to make none to me. Break from the reservation if you want. Fight if you want. Fight until you know that there is no use fighting any longer because when you kill a soldier, ten more will come, and twenty the next time. How many Apaches will you bring for the ones you lose?" He turned back and sat down, waiting for the Apache to speak. Then he looked at Moses. "Isn't he going to say anything?"

"What is there to say, sir? He knows how it is."

"All right, put him with the others, then." He waved his hand and the guards moved Cochise to the roped-in area. Fickland glanced at his officers. "I'll expect full reports by sundown. You might as well start details back with the wounded." He rubbed his hands across his eyes and pulled a canvas-bottomed camp stool around for Moses. "Sit down, Sergeant. I'll listen to your report now; I know you didn't ride to Railey's for the exercise."

Joe Moses knew what Fickland wanted, the skeleton of facts, and he made the whole thing brief. "Lieutenant Baker is in command of the detail, sir. His report —"

Fickland waved his hand. "Yes, yes, he'll write six pages." He got up and stretched. "You might as well return to the post with Baker's detail, Sergeant. At his convenience."

"Yes, sir." He hesitated. "Sir, I didn't see Captain Dane."

"He's with the wounded," Fickland said, frowning. "I'm afraid it's a pension out for George. He went down in our first brush with the Apaches. Horse crushed his leg. The surgeon amputated above the knee." He glanced at Moses. "You'll be getting back before the wounded. Tell his wife."

"Yes, sir," Moses said.

"Moses, do you know why I'm giving

you that job? I want you to see for yourself that it wouldn't work out."

"Why wouldn't it, Major?"

"God knows why," Fickland said. "I saw what was going on and I kept my mouth shut because I know you, Joe. I wish I could make you a second lieutenant."

"She wouldn't leave him now," he said and walked to his horse.

He sat in her quarters, his hat balanced on his knees, and watched her cry and he wondered if she cried because their love was lost or because George Dane who dreamed so much and so big would spend the rest of his life a cripple.

The boys were away, playing in the stable yard, watching the remount detail work. Finally she wiped her eyes and said, "When are the wagons due in?"

"Day after tomorrow," he said. "Maybe the next day." He got up and held his hat. "Good-bye, Mildred."

She stared at him. "Is that all? Is that all we get?"

"What else is there? If you were anything less than you are you'd — But you're not different, and that's why I love you." He took her hand and held it, standing close to her. "A kiss would be nice but that's all it would take to put me on my knees begging you to let him go his own way while you went mine."

"For the rest of my life, Joe, I'll —"

"I know. The same with me."

He turned quickly to the door and went out, walking hurriedly across the parade ground.

An hour later he had his buggy hitched and was on the way to Tucson to get the mail. There he met Al Roan, who was very glad to see Moses; they went to the jail and Roan released Pete Ketchel, whose red eyes attested that he had been on one hell of a drunk.

"Joe, old friend. Oh, you're a sight."

"Let's go for a buggy ride," Moses said.

"Just the thing," Pete said, gathering his coat and hat. In the outer office, Roan handed him his pistol belt and personal effects. "Did I give you a rough time, Marshal?"

"You were nice about it, Pete. I only had to hit you once."

Ketchel shook his head. "I must be slippin'. That's what bein' rich does to a man."

He went outside and got into Moses' buggy and they drove out of town.

They camped that night on the road, made a fire for the meal, then because they were careful men who understood that trouble was never really far away, spread their blankets away from the fire and slept with their weapons close by.

Moses found sleep difficult. He had things to think about, things he tried not to think about; but trying only brought them nearer. He heard Pete Ketchel stirring and said, "What's the matter with you? You give up sleep?"

"I'm a rich man," Ketchel said. "And I'm alone, Joe. God, I can't get used to that." He sat up. "I guess that's why I got drunk, because I knew I'd have to go it alone. A man needs a partner."

"That's a fact," Moses said, but putting a different meaning on it.

"You'll be out of a job soon," Pete said. "Roan told me that the stage was making up for the run to Lordsburg. The fireman's band was going to play in front of the hotel and there was going to be free beer to celebrate. Now that the road's open —"

"Everything changes. A man's got to expect that."

Ketchel fell silent for a time. "Joe, would you consider coming in with me? Right down the line, a fifty-fifty split?" He waited a moment. "I'm cold sober, Joe. You know that. There isn't another man I respect more than you, or another I like as well. Joe, will you think about it?"

"Yes," Moses said. "Get some sleep."

Moses reached Lordsburg on a Friday, the third day out of Tucson; he had made his usual good time. He put up at the hotel, made the rounds to see his friends, and had his drink in George Howard's saloon. In a half hour the news of the army's battle with the Apaches was all over town and there was celebrating in the streets until very late that night.

Even the arrival of the Tucson stage, and in record time, failed to tarnish the celebration. The livery stable owner sold every horse he owned before nine the next morning, and by noon he had sold a few whose ownership was questionable. The town was emptying of people and wagons and they were all moving west along the road.

Moses slept until noon, then checked at the express office. Harry Spears was there and he grinned and spread his hands. "Military dispatches only, Joe. The mail went out on the stage."

"Progress, there's no stopping it," Moses said and went to the barbershop for a shave and a haircut.

He was having his meal in the hote
when the clerk came in, sought him out
and said, "Joe, there's a woman who wants
a ride back to Tucson."

He looked up from his stew and tomatoes. "You tell her to take the stage."

"Room eleven at the end of the hall
street side," the clerk said. "She told me to
tell you that."

Pete Ketchel came in then and straddled a
chair and the clerk went away. He put his hat
on the table and said, "Boy, is money easy to
get when you're rich. I figured it out and ten
thousand ought to get us well started. I'm
countin' on you, Joe. Can I do that?"

"This is my last run, I guess," Moses
said. "It may take me a week to get out,
papers and everything."

"Hell, what's a week?" Ketchel said, and
laughed and slapped himself on the rib cage.
"Joe, maybe you won't understand this, but
right now, this minute, is the first time I felt
like laughin' since Jim died. We're goin' to
get along, Joe. You know that?"

"You're a good man, Pete. A damned
good man."

"How's the stew?"

"Mexican beef," Moses said, finishing
his coffee. "Try it."

"Who has a choice?"

276

Moses laid a quarter on the table and walked out to the lobby. He started for the street door then thought of what the clerk had said, and turned up the broad stairs and walked to room eleven.

He knocked. Mildred Dane opened the door and he stared at her then stepped inside without a word. After she closed the door, she said, "Four hours after you left the post, Lieutenant Travis came back. I'm alone, Joe."

"George didn't make it?"

She shook her head. "You're sorry, aren't you?"

"Yes."

"Joe, we didn't buy anything at his expense. Understand that because I've thought of nothing else on the stage. George was what he wanted to be, a hero. Take me back with you."

He shook his head. "I'm not going back to stay. You wait for me here."

"But — I don't understand."

He put his arms around her. "Well, I'll have the rest of my life to tell you about it, so what's the hurry." Then he laughed softly; it was a bubble in him, alive and full and he knew that tomorrow would be a shining, exciting day.

We hope you have enjoyed this Large Print book. Other Thorndike, Wheeler or Chivers Press Large Print books are available at your library or directly from the publishers.

For more information about current and upcoming titles, please call or write, without obligation, to:

Publisher
Thorndike Press
295 Kennedy Memorial Drive
Waterville, ME   04901
Tel. (800) 223-1244

Or visit our Web site at:
www.gale.com/thorndike
www.gale.com/wheeler

OR

Chivers Large Print
published by BBC Audiobooks Ltd
St James House, The Square
Lower Bristol Road
Bath BA2 3BH
England
Tel. +44(0) 800 136919
email: bbcaudiobooks@bbc.co.uk
www.bbcaudiobooks.co.uk

All our Large Print titles are designed for easy reading, and all our books are made to last.